Sam in Winter

Sam in Winter

Edward van de Vendel

Illustrated by
Philip Hopman

Translated by
David Colmer

Eerdmans Books for Young Readers
Grand Rapids, Michigan

Eerdmans Books for Young Readers,
an imprint of
Wm. B. Eerdmans Publishing Co.
2140 Oak Industrial Drive N.E., Grand Rapids, Michigan 49505
www.eerdmans.com/youngreaders

Published in 2017 by Eerdmans Books for Young Readers

Originally published as *De raadsels van Sam* by
Em. Querido's Kinderboeken Uitgeverij
Text © 2012 Edward van de Vendel
Illustrations © 2012 Philip Hopman

Printed in the United States of America

23 22 21 20 19 18 17   1 2 3 4 5 6 7

ISBN 978-0-8028-5487-2

A catalog listing is available from the Library of Congress.

N **ederlands**
letterenfonds
dutch foundation
for literature

The publisher gratefully acknowledges the support
of the Dutch Foundation for Literature.

Sam in Winter

1

It was nighttime.

Kix was already in bed, waiting to fall asleep and hoping he'd have some good dreams. Moonlight was shining through the curtains, reflected up off the snow.

He wondered when he would be too old to be read to. With luck it wouldn't be any time soon, because his mother had just started a new book about Bunnicula, the vampire rabbit. The Bunnicula books were the funniest books Kix knew. There was a whole series of them. Nine and a half wasn't too old for bedtime stories, was it?

After that Kix thought about Sam, of course.

Sam was the dog that had shown up at the start of summer and decided he wanted to be Kix's dog. And Emilia's dog too, at least partly. Emilia was Kix's little sister. Sam had been at their place ever since.

He was a mysterious dog. Last week, when Kix and his mom were trying to get the knots out of Sam's long white hair, they discovered that he had twenty-two toes. Five on each of his front paws, like there were supposed to be, but six on each of his hind legs.

"Is that normal for mountain dogs?" Kix asked his mother. She didn't know.

It was another one of Sam's mysteries.

Kix listened for any sound of howling. That was something Sam did every night when trains went by in the distance. They blew their horns at the bend, and Sam howled along in tune.

Often his howls had a secret meaning, a message for Kix. Kix had never told anyone that, but he knew it was true.

Sometimes Sam was just saying *Goodnight*, but sometimes he was telling Kix that he was happy here on their little farm. That he was friends with the horses. And with Springer and Holly, the other dogs.

Sometimes Sam was saying *Sorry*. Sorry that he'd spent the night somewhere else. Because Sam did that sometimes. He was an outdoor dog, and he decided for himself where to sleep and where to live. Kix knew that things like that weren't up to him.

But now he heard a different kind of howling.

Kix recognized it and shot up in bed. He'd been expecting this: it was still a long way off, but it was definitely coyotes.

Coyotes usually kept a safe distance from farms, but sometimes they came closer and tried to steal a chicken or a rabbit at night. They looked like little wolves and they yowled, *ulululululuuu* — and now the cold wind was carrying that sound to Kix's bedroom.

It sounded scary and spooky, but Kix didn't really need to be afraid of coyotes, because they wouldn't eat people. And Kix's farm didn't have any chickens or rabbits.

Plus, when the coyotes crossed the tracks, Dad would go out with the big flashlight and shine it in their eyes. They didn't like that, and then they'd run for it: *ulululululuuuu!*

This year they were coming pretty close. Because of the early winter, they were even hungrier and bolder than usual. At breakfast the last couple of days, Dad had said he'd gone out at night to scare them off.

Ulululululuuuu!

Kix was disappointed that he'd slept through it till now. But tonight he heard them. They were yowling and yowling, and it sounded mean and cruel.

Kix jumped out of bed and ran to his bedroom door.

Dad was in the hall pulling on his coat. He saw Kix and said firmly, "Stay inside, Kix!"

"But . . ."

"No."

Kix went back to his bedroom and pushed open the curtains.

There was his dad. He was walking toward the edge of the field behind their house, holding the giant flashlight and a piece of wood.

Kix felt his heart start to pound, because he'd spotted them. He could see the coyotes! There were five of them, maybe six. They were loping along quite far away, but they were getting closer.

Dad raised the flashlight and shone it straight at their heads.

But why did they keep coming? Why didn't the light stop them like it usually did? And the coyotes weren't howling anymore either. They were making a very different sound. They were yelping, as if they were in pain.

Kix stood on tiptoe. Why had Dad taken that piece of wood with him? Was he scared he'd have to defend himself? Did coyotes sometimes attack people after all? Not usually, but tonight?

Suddenly he started shivering in his pajamas. He wanted to open the window and yell to Dad to come back in. But then he saw that the coyotes had stopped after all. They didn't dare come any closer.

And he saw that they'd formed a circle about fifty or sixty feet away from Dad.

A circle around something. Around a dog.

Around Sam.

Sam! It was like a hammer. As if someone had suddenly hit Kix with a hammer, right on his head. Because all of a sudden he remembered that once, a long time ago, a dog had been attacked. In the middle of the day. A pack of coyotes had snatched a stray puppy from the dog park in town. Kix had forgotten all about that. Sam was big and strong, but there were six coyotes here, *six*!

The coyotes were squeaking and yelping louder than ever and making wild jumps. They were all around Sam, just a few steps away from him, lunging at him with one twisting leap after the other.

It was like they'd gone crazy. Driven mad by the beam of Dad's flashlight. And by Sam.

Kix didn't know what to do. Was there another piece of wood somewhere? Then he could go and stand next to his dad. Or wait — what about Dad's gun? Where was that — where did he keep it hidden?

But then it happened.

Sam had been sitting there quietly the whole time. Relaxed. Calmly watching the jittery coyotes. Then all at once he stood up, as if he'd had enough.

He barked. Once. Loudly.

Again. Just as loud.

The coyotes flinched, and within a second they shot off. Yelping, scared. Almost out of sight already.

6

Sam was the boss. Maybe he'd already chased off a million coyotes in his lifetime. He toyed with them for a while, laughing to himself while he let them come closer, and then, when he was sick of it: *woof*, enough!

It was fantastic.

Dad came in shaking his head and asked, "Did you see that?"

"Yes," Kix whispered. He was so proud of his dog he could hardly speak.

Dad laughed, "I bet we won't see another coyote here all winter."

2

The next morning at breakfast, Kix told Emilia how Sam had defeated the coyotes. Dad had already gone to work, and Mom was making herself some coffee.

"It was a miracle," Kix said. "Those coyotes just took off."

Emilia thought for a moment. She had some Nutella on her lip. "It wasn't a miracle," she said. "That was Sam's job, wasn't it? Chasing off wild animals?"

Emilia was right.

Sam had worked on a farm in the mountains his whole life. He'd slept next to the horses and guarded the sheep. He'd chased away wolves. And coyotes too, of course.

The farmer who owned Sam was called Flint. But the farm went bankrupt, and Flint had to sell all of his sheep and horses. Only Sam was left.

Then something terrible happened. Losing his farm made Flint so desperate that he kicked Sam. His own faithful dog!

Kix had heard about it from Grandpa, and Grandpa had heard it from other people — but it was true, because afterward Flint went to a hospital for people with mental problems.

For a while Sam was too scared to walk over to people who were standing up straight. If you wanted to pet him, you had to kneel down so he could see you weren't going to kick him.

Flint's parents took Sam to their house, which was across the road from Kix's. But Sam didn't want to stay there. The very next day he ambled over to Kix and Emilia's house. He saw the horses and dogs and decided that from then on he had a new herd. He wanted to belong to Kix and Emilia, and he wanted to protect them.

He stayed all summer. He stayed all fall. And now Kix could talk with Sam as if they were friends. Like they were two boys, or two dogs, or maybe something in between.

Kix told everyone at school about the coyotes. He didn't exaggerate on purpose, but the story did get a little bit better each time he told it. With a few extra coyotes howling a little bit closer to his bedroom window. That didn't matter. Kix's friends loved Sam too.

That afternoon, when they came over to play, they petted Sam twice as long, because now he wasn't just big, beautiful, and friendly — he was brave too.

They all went to the campground. They'd been doing that almost every day since it started snowing.

The campground was right next to Kix's farm. And when the town plows cleared snow, they always dumped it on the field they used for tents and campers in summer. Now there were mountains there, mountains of snow.

Kix and Emilia had no fewer than four good toboggans, and they used them to go screaming down the snowy hills.

Sam was there too.

That afternoon Sam played like a puppy. He was an old

dog, ten at least, but ever since there'd been a chill in the air, he'd shown that he could still act like Springer sometimes. He rolled on his back, snorted, and sprayed ice-cold snowy droplets everywhere. Everyone laughed, and Mom took pictures and videos with her cell phone.

But toward the end of the afternoon something strange happened, something Kix had noticed a few times before. All of a sudden, Sam stopped playing. He just stood there staring at the snow. Or at the sky. Sam was still strong and kind, but if you looked closely, you could see something pale in his eyes. No, not *in* his eyes — behind them.

His friends kept throwing snowballs, but Kix went over to Sam and knelt down on the ground in front of him. His knees got cold, but that didn't matter.

Kix pulled off his mittens and petted his wonder dog. Sam had a very broad forehead — you could almost rest a plate on it. Every morning before breakfast, Kix would go outside, and then Sam would lower his head a little and press that big forehead against one of Kix's legs. That meant, *Pet me. Pet me, Kix.*

"Sam, Sam, Sammy boy," Kix said, scratching under Sam's ears the way he always did. First one side, then the other. Often Sam would start groaning, he loved it so much.

But now he stayed quiet.

Kix moved his hands back to the first ear, then rubbed all over Sam's head, then leaned forward and buried his nose in Sam's fluffy white fur.

"Sam, Sam, Sammy boy," Kix said again, "Don't you want to go for another roll in the snow?"

And finally, at last, Sam nodded. Without moving his

head. He nodded inside his head. *Okay then, Kix,* he seemed to say, *if it makes you happy . . .*

3

That evening, just before supper, Kix asked his mother if she'd noticed it too.

"What do you mean?" Mom asked.

Kix explained, and then she sat down across from him at the kitchen table and said, "Sam is old. You know that. And old dogs have a whole lifetime behind them. They're not as easy to understand as little Springer. Yesterday Sam was looking at the gate. The horse gate. I opened it, but then he just kept looking. It was like he couldn't decide what to do about the gate. Do you mean things like that?"

That was the kind of thing Kix meant. More or less.

Kix kept thinking about it, and that night in bed, he said, "Mom, do you think it's the cold? Sam's always outside, day and night. And there are all kinds of cracks in the shed wall. The door doesn't even shut. Maybe Sam gets a bit frozen sometimes. On the inside."

Mom pressed her hands against Kix's cheeks.

"Honey," she said, "Sam likes the cold. And mountain dogs have a double coat. There's a layer of air between the first layer of hair and the second layer, and that air keeps them cool in summer and warm in winter. Once I heard a story about a lady who shaved her dog for the summer. She thought it would be nice and cool. But the poor dog almost dropped dead because of the heat."

"How?" said Kix. "I don't get it."

"Me neither, not entirely, but Sam's fine in the snow. Maybe he's just a little tired. Like you are right now. Shall we read a bit? *Bunnicula?*"

After a couple of chapters, Kix got a goodnight kiss from his mom, who closed his bedroom door. Kix stared up at the glow-in-the-dark stars on the ceiling.

So Sam's got a fur coat, he thought.

It made him laugh.

And when he thought about the coyotes from the night before, he had to laugh again.

He yawned.

Sam was the kind of dog that kept you guessing. Holly, his mother's dog, only ever wanted to sleep. She was always calm. Springer, his father's pup, only ever wanted to play. She was always excited. But Sam was full of surprises.

Like at the end of summer, when he suddenly didn't like cars going away anymore. He'd always lie down in front of them, in the middle of the driveway, or even out on the road.

And now Sam lay there on the gravel every morning when Kix's dad wanted to go to work. Dad had no choice but to get out of the pickup and go talk to him.

After a while, Sam would haul himself up onto his feet, and when Kix saw Sam do that, he always thought he could hear him mumbling something like, *Okay, okay, if you insist . . .*

One day someone came to check the furnace and honked when he wanted to drive off. "What's that mutt doing there?" he shouted. He'd rolled his window down, and clouds of angry steam were coming out of his mouth.

14

Kix ran over, lured Sam away from the driveway, and called out, "This dog is named Sam, and he lies down wherever he wants to."

"Bah!" the repairman yelled, roaring off.

Kix laughed for the third time. Quietly. He was almost asleep. But he still had just enough time to think, *Sam's quiet moods aren't that bad. They're part of him. I've got a dog who's always different. I've got a dog everyone wants — but he chose me.*

4

A few weeks later, Kix's dad moved the horses around to the strip of land behind the house. The wind wasn't quite as cutting there, and Jill and Study and Patriot could go into the stable themselves if it got stormy or started to snow too hard.

Sam was almost always near them. Sometimes, when Kix went to have a look, the four of them were just staring into space. At other times it looked like they were whispering animal jokes to each other.

The winter kept getting colder. Halfway through November, it was already below zero, so Kix and his father tried to make a little house for Sam. They stacked up bales of straw to make the walls and laid the cushions from Sam's old sofa between them.

But their work was wasted, because Sam never slept in it once. Instead, he moved into the stable, so Dad lugged the cushions over to the stable and laid some extra straw on the floor.

It got colder and colder. The temperature fell so low that Mom bought blankets for the horses. Kix and Emilia helped lay them over the horses' backs. Sam looked on from a distance and sniffed the air.

"Yes, Sam," Mom said, "there really is too much snow. It hasn't been this deep for a few years now, so maybe we need to try to protect you too."

"How?" Emilia asked. "Are we going to put a blanket on his back?"

"No," Mom said, "I was thinking of the garage."

"It won't work," said Kix. "He won't like that."

"We'll see," said Mom.

She made a little palace for Sam in a corner of the garage with his cushions and two old blankets. Kix and Emilia lugged a bale of straw in too, and Mom cooked Sam's favorite food: meat with vegetables and a bone.

She made sure that Holly and Springer couldn't steal any of it and left the side door slightly open.

Sam had sat on the garage step plenty of times, but he had never gone further. Sometimes it was like he didn't know how to come in, and sometimes Kix thought he couldn't believe he was allowed in. That he was convinced the garage was different from the stable, field, and yard, and it could never belong to him too.

But would Sam understand what they'd done for him now?

Kix had to call him ten times. He squatted down, just inside the door, and reached out to Sam like he had in those first few weeks, when Sam wouldn't come to you unless you were the same height as him.

Mom waved the food bowl in the air to get the smell wafting out to Sam's nose.

And then, finally, Sam came in.

Kix had been sure Sam wouldn't let himself be lured in, but slowly, hesitantly, step by step, they managed to get Sam into his palace.

"For the king!" Emilia called out, when Sam sniffed at his bed. "For you!"

Mom quickly closed the door.

Kix begged and begged until his parents let him eat his spaghetti next to Sam. Emilia came along too, but after five minutes she went back to the kitchen for more ketchup and didn't come back.

It wasn't that easy, trying to get a mouthful of spaghetti into his mouth with one hand, while stroking the snowy hair of Sam, King of the Dogs, with the other. And for dessert Kix had to go back and eat at the table.

But he didn't get time to be upset about it, because Sam started bellowing.

It was like someone had turned on a siren.

They all ran to the garage.

Sam was standing at the garage door with his snout in the air, howling and scratching, his claws rattling over the metal.

Mom tried to calm him down. She stroked him under one ear, but it didn't help. *Hoooooooee!* went Sam, *hoooooooee!*

Kix ran over to press the switch for the door, which rose slowly with a buzzing sound.

Sam bent down, sniffed at the gap of air that had appeared and slipped out into the twenty-below air of early December as soon as he fit through.

Dad sighed, "You could have just opened the side door, Kix. Now all the heat's gone."

Kix didn't care. He had pressed the button a second time and the door was already moving down again. He'd had a good view of Sam jumping into the snow.

Mom said, "You were right, Kix. He didn't like it. He's not used to being inside."

Dad said, "He missed the horses."

"No," said Emilia, "he just didn't want to be a king."

5

It was a couple of weeks into the new year, and still freezing cold. Everyone was tired of all that snow. Every day they looked up at the sky, hoping for a chinook. That was a kind of storm, with a strong wind that was a lot warmer than the usual winter air.

You could see a chinook coming. All of the clouds seemed to lie down next to each other in a row, as if they were making a bridge, a white arch over the mountains. The bridge of clouds was the first sign of a chinook, and when the wind started blowing it melted all the snow. Even if the snow was three feet deep, within a day it would be gone.

The First Nations said "the big ice-eater is coming," and Kix thought that was a really beautiful way of putting it.

On the day the big ice-eater finally cleared the snow off the grass, Kix and Emilia jumped out of Mom's big new car. They rode home with her because she worked at their school — she was the music teacher.

Kix went looking for his dog. "Sam?" he called. "Sam?"

Sam usually appeared right away. Sam recognized all the cars by sound, Dad's and Grandpa's too.

"Sam?"

It wasn't until he'd called a few times that the white dog came wobbling up. Emilia skipped into the house to see Springer, but Mom locked the car, looked at Sam, and said, "What's the matter with him?"

Kix saw it too. Sam was limping.

No, he wasn't limping. He was walking slowly, stiffly. As if his legs were made of wood.

"Sam?" Kix asked, running over to his dog. "What's wrong?" Sam stopped just in front of Kix and shook his head so hard his ears flapped. That meant, *Huh? I'm fine.*

And to everyone's relief, Sam was back to normal again a little later.

But Kix knew what he had seen. And Mom knew too. They talked to Dad about it. And when Patriot cut himself that weekend on an old haymaking machine and needed stitches, Dad asked the vet, "What do we do if he gets sick?" He pointed at Sam. "We can't get him into a car. He decides for himself where he wants to go."

"Hmm," said the vet. "Normally people have to bring their dogs into the clinic. I guess I can come by if it's really necessary. But why? Is something wrong with him?"

"No, not now," Dad said. "He was limping the other day, and after a while it went away. But he never lets us get close to his paws. Not even to just feel them."

"I'd have to sedate him," the vet said. "That can be quite hard on a dog. It could make him feel pretty sick."

"It's not necessary right now," said Dad.

"Old bones," the vet said, as she was getting back into her car. She looked at Sam. "But he's a tough one, by the looks of him. He'll hang in there for a good while yet."

Dad nodded. And Kix, who was standing next to Dad, nodded too.

Still, Kix was worried more and more often. Because although Sam was still strong and brave and sweet, strange things kept happening.

"Sam is such a deep sleeper," Mom said one day. "Sometimes I clap my hands right next to his ears, and he just keeps on snoring."

Kix had noticed that too. Usually he saw Sam's tail wagging from side to side like a waving flag the moment he stepped into the stable. Sam would hear the snow crunching under Kix's boots. *Kix!* Sam's tail wagged. *Kix!*

But now and then there was no tail-wagging at all, and definitely no *Kix*ing. And even after Kix knelt down next to Sam and started to comb his hair with his fingers, even after Patriot and the others had neighed good morning, Sam would still lie there dreaming.

"Is he sick?" Kix asked.

"I wish I knew," Mom said. "I don't really think so. Because then he'd be slow like that all the time, instead of just now and then. It must be old age. Or another one of his mysteries."

Kix sighed. "Maybe he needs some kind of medicine."

"Medicine for mysteriousness?" Mom laughed.

"Mo-omm!"

"Sorry."

6

Maybe there wasn't any need for all that worrying? The next few days Sam was in a good mood again. He played knock-'em-over with Springer and had fun diving into the snow. He teased Dad by lying down in front of his car, and he did it to Grandpa too. They had to get out and explain why they wanted to get past. Sometimes Sam was so happy he even squeaked, like a puppy.

Medicine? That was silly. If Sam needed something, he would take care of it himself.

And he did. That very weekend.

With a special kind of medicine.

Sometimes other dogs came to visit Sam. A while back it had been two big Saint Bernards. All of a sudden they were wandering around the field, and it was like the horses already knew them and were introducing them to Sam. "Here," they whinnied, "this is Tom, and this is Jerry. They're nice guys — maybe you can be friends."

Kix was watching. Sam had been quite cool with them at first, but an hour later the three of them were walking across the field together. When Kix rattled Sam's food bowl a bit later, the two dogs were already gone — they were strays who made up their own minds about when to come and when to go.

Since then there hadn't been many visitors, but on the last Saturday in January, Kix went into the stable and saw Choca lying there.

He didn't know what she was really called, but Kix thought that was a good name for Sam's new girlfriend.

She was a brown Labrador, and there was no tag on her collar.

She came and stayed, and she and Sam spent the whole time cuddling.

Kix had never seen his dog do anything like that before. Sam rolled over onto his side and tapped Choca with his paws. She jumped over his big white body and buried her face in the fur under his neck. Sam turned his head toward her and pretended to take a bite out of her snout. Choca snapped back, and sometimes they kept playing for five minutes or more before they even noticed Kix was there.

So it went all Saturday, and Sunday too, and it made Mom and Kix and Emilia happy to watch.

"Sam's in love," said Emilia.

"In love at his age," Mom said.

In love — Kix thought it was a silly, girlish thing to say, but that really was what it looked like. And during Sunday supper, when Dad said that keeping three dogs really was the maximum, and that if Choca was still there in the morning, they'd have to ask around town to see if anyone had lost a dark-brown Labrador, Kix said, "Dad, Sam's groaning all day long. Normally he only does that if you pet him under his ears. Don't you get it? They're in love!"

Going steady or mystery medicine, it didn't matter what you called it. Monday afternoon when Kix got home from school, Sam and Choca were still romping around. At night they howled at the train together, and Kix understood the message Sam sent him in the middle of his howling: *Kix, what do you think? Isn't she beauuuuuutiful?*

7

And then she was gone. Just like that.

On Tuesday morning Sam was lying on his cushions alone.

"Sam?" Kix asked. He'd brought a handful of dog treats with him. Twice as many as normal, enough for Choca too. "Where is she?"

Kix knelt down next to his dog. Sam didn't react — he just kept lying there. "Sam? Did you two have a fight?"

Kix rubbed Sam's back and ruffled the hair on his side. "Do you want a treat, Sam?"

No, Sam didn't want any treats. He glanced up at Kix for a moment, but it was like his eyes couldn't be bothered to look anymore. They were tired, and there wasn't any message in them at all. Sam let his head droop again, as far as it would go, with one ear pressed against the ground.

Kix had never seen his dog as happy as he'd been the last few days, but he'd never seen him this exhausted either.

Mom called out that Kix had to hurry to get ready for school, but Kix yelled back, "Mom, quick, come here!"

They sat next to Sam for a while, listening to him sigh.

"I don't think there's anything wrong with him," Mom said. "Not physically, I mean."

"It's because of Choca," said Kix.

"Yes," said Mom. "But he'll forget about her soon. Dogs forget quickly. You know what? I'll take you and Emilia to school, and then I'll keep an eye on him for the rest of the day."

"What if he doesn't get over it?"

"He will. Grandpa will be here soon. I'll get him to take a look at Sam. And if there's no improvement, we'll call the vet. But it's silly to think like that now. He's just having a bad day. And maybe his little girlfriend will come back again. Later. *Tralala*, everything will be fine."

Kix petted Sam one more time on the top of his flat head. "I hope so, Mom. I really do."

But he didn't believe that Sam was going to go *tralala* at all. On the way to school, he stared out of the window, and during recess he discovered something in his coat pocket.

A handful of dog treats.

After school, things were a bit better. Choca hadn't come back, but Sam was walking around the edges of the field. He did that a couple of times a week. Going on patrol, like a soldier. He'd check the fields and the whole farm and wouldn't lie down again until he'd made sure everything was okay.

Now he wasn't marching along with his usual determination, and his tail wasn't sticking up as proudly either. He'd also stopped a couple of times to sniff the air, as if he'd lost his way and had to check where Kix lived. But at least he was doing something. He wasn't just lying there limply on the straw.

"See?" Mom said. "He's almost forgotten Choca already."

Kix lowered his binoculars. "Did Grandpa come?"

"Yes," said Mom.

"What did he say?"

"Oh, you know. That Sam is an old dog, but strong. That maybe he's a little bit confused now, but . . ."

Mom didn't go on.

"What?" said Kix.

"Well, it is a bit of a hassle to have the vet come. And Sam *has* stopped limping . . ."

Kix had to agree with her about that. Sam *had* stopped dragging his legs.

But early in the evening, Sam started whining. It wasn't like his usual howl. It was a very quiet whine. Sad whimpering.

Kix heard it when he was taking some carrots out to the horses. Apparently Sam had crept to the back of the stable, somewhere between a pile of wood and couple of old bales of hay.

How had he found his way into the back corner like that? It was almost completely blocked off. It was as if he'd gotten lost in there.

After a lot of calling and begging, Kix got Sam back out. "Here I am, come on," he said. "Sammy-Sam, here, don't cry."

But Sam kept on making those mournful sounds. Kix fetched Mom and Dad and Emilia, and together they petted him and tried to figure out what it could be.

"Maybe he does have a broken heart," said Mom.

"It's the long winter," said Dad.

"Toothache," said Emilia.

That made Kix angry. "Don't be stupid," he snapped at his sister, and then Mom said that fighting wasn't going to make things any better.

"Things?" Kix said, getting even angrier, because Sam wasn't a thing. "There's something wrong, and I'm staying with Sam until he gets better, and tomorrow the vet has to come."

After Kix said that, Mom petted *him*. She stroked the back of his head and told Dad, "He's right. We'll call the vet in the morning."

"Yes," Dad said, "okay."

And then Kix wasn't quite so angry. But even one day of not understanding his dog was too much to take — one day of not having any dog thoughts lighting up in his brain.

They sat there for another quarter of an hour, but then they were able to go back inside. Sam had fallen asleep. And Mom promised to go and check on him every half hour.

Soon after that it was Emilia's bedtime, and then Kix's.

"*Bunnicula?*" asked Mom after he'd brushed his teeth.

"No," said Kix, "not tonight."

8

Mysteries. They kept appearing when Sam was around. Sometimes there were even new ones two days in a row.

On the first of those two days, the day after Sam's big, sad whimpering fit, everything seemed better again. Sam was back to his old self. It was as if a chinook had melted his sadness away. His eyes were clear again, as clear as the blue sky over the mountains. He wagged his tail when Kix came out of the house, got up off his cushions, and was even happy and playful enough to take something in his mouth, something he'd picked off the workbench.

"What have you got there, boy?" Kix asked. "Silly dog, what is it?"

It was the brush Kix and Mom and Emilia had bought that summer, just after Sam had moved into their old horse shed. Every week they'd used it to brush the tangles out of his coat, and Sam had stood there almost trembling with pleasure.

They hadn't gotten around to giving him a good brushing since Christmas vacation, and Kix had actually thought that Sam could use all of those knots and tufts of loose hair in his coat to protect him from the cold. It had started snowing again, and they'd left the brush lying there to wait for spring and warm weather.

"Do you want to be brushed again now? Even though it's still winter?" Kix asked.

Sam's tail started wagging even more furiously.

Kix went straight to work. He dug the brush into Sam's thick coat and teased out the white clumps. It was fantastic, because he understood his dog again! He had to go to school, but in the afternoon he got back to it, and kept going until the stable was half full of little clouds and balls of white hair. And the vet could stay home because Sam's sorrow was gone and forgotten, and he wasn't limping anymore either.

Then evening fell, and it was night, and Kix heard, *Hoooot! Hoooooeet!!* The sound came from the trains in the dark and Sam's howling. Everything was just the way it should be.

But the next morning Sam didn't come out to meet him when Kix wanted to start the day by petting him. And there was no sound of Sam from the stable.

Because he wasn't there at all.

Sam was gone.

9

Yes, Sam was gone, and Kix stood in the stable for ten whole minutes looking out over the fields, and he didn't like it at all. He didn't like having to search for his dog, calling out "Sam! Sam! Sam!" But it had happened plenty of times before. Sam went away and Sam came back.

Mom said what she always said: "Don't worry. He'll be back tomorrow. Or the next day."

That afternoon, after school, Kix and his grandpa went in to town. Grandpa was trading his old Chevy in for a new one.

"Sam's gone!" Kix told Grandpa.

"Oh," Grandpa laughed. "Did he get itchy feet again? Off on a field trip?"

And that was pretty funny. Sam on a field trip! They went on those at school sometimes: visiting the birds of prey center, or going to the river, canoeing. Ha! Sam in a canoe.

But it really wasn't funny, because the next day Sam was still gone, and the morning after too, and even the morning after that.

Kix had gotten up extra early. Emilia was still asleep. Dad had already gone to work, and Mom was checking her email.

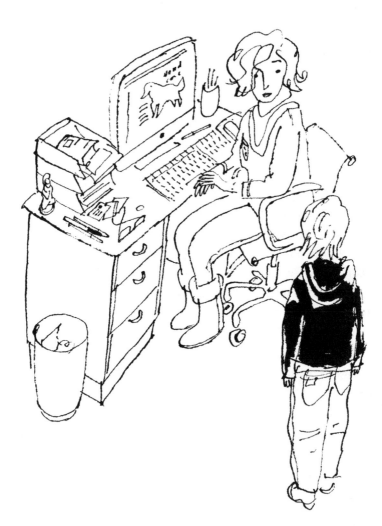

"He must be back by now," Kix said to Mom's back as he ran past. He didn't stop, because he'd had uneasy dreams all night. "I'm gonna have a look. He has to be there this time."

Mom turned around and said something, but Kix didn't hear it — he was already halfway out the door.

Sam was nowhere to be seen.

Kix ran back in, shouting, "He's not there! He should've been back by now."

Mom got up from her desk. "I know. I've already checked too."

"Yeah, but how can he be gone this long?" Kix said. "He's never stayed away this many nights!"

He had to do his best not to start shouting. How could his mother sit there reading emails when Sam had been missing for three days already?

"Come here," Mom said, pulling him toward the computer. "If he's not back by this afternoon, we'll start looking. Okay? We'll go for a drive. Maybe he's rummaging around somewhere or off playing with other dogs. And if we don't find him, we'll make something like this." Mom pointed at the screen. "What do you think?"

It said LOST DOG in thick black letters above a photo of Sam.

"Were you . . ." said Kix. "Weren't you reading your email?"

"Honey, no — I'm trying to make a poster to hang up if Sam's really . . . well . . . he'll probably be snuffling around the lawn again later."

Mom sounded serious. Her cheeks were red — were they redder than usual?

"How long have you been up?" Kix asked.

"I couldn't sleep."

"Mom, how long?"

"Oh, I'm not sure. Three or four hours?"

That really gave Kix a shock. His mother had been up thinking about Sam for three whole hours. Because he was missing.

"Mom!" Kix blurted, "I don't want this! He can't be lost!"

10

Kix's teacher was a good teacher. His friends were good friends. And the other kids weren't nearly as annoying today as they could be sometimes. But Kix just couldn't pay attention. Not to his teacher or his friends, not to anyone at all. He tried to block out his thoughts — Sam with a broken leg, Sam in a ditch, Sam hit by a truck, Sam whimpering, Sam whining, Sam on his back, completely alone — but he couldn't. And he felt like he was acting like a baby, because for all he knew, Sam would be back walking between the horse's legs when Kix and Mom and Emilia turned into the driveway after school.

But when they did turn onto the crunching gravel that afternoon, there was no sign of Sam at all.

They were sitting at the kitchen table. Dad had left to go to a construction site, but Mom told them that he had spent the whole afternoon searching for Sam.

"Dad spent hours walking through the cold," Mom said. "But the snow had covered up any tracks. Then he went to the neighbors' across the road and a few other farms, but nobody's seen Sam. He checked along the tracks and at the campground. But now he's gone back to work, and we have to make a plan. What are we going to do?"

"That poster," Kix said. "We have to stick it up everywhere."

"We'll take a plane," Emilia said, looking very serious. "And then we'll hover over the fields and call out, 'Sam, Sam, Sa-am!'"

Sometimes Kix felt like punching his little sister. Like now. The only reason he didn't was because he knew it wouldn't help.

"Choca!" he said suddenly.

"What?" said Mom.

"That's it! He's gone to visit Choca! I bet she lives somewhere nearby. If we find her, we'll find Sam."

It was all clear in his head. That was the explanation. Why hadn't he thought of it before?

"Come on, Mom," he said. "Have you already printed the poster? Maybe we won't even need it. What are you waiting for? Emilia, put on your coat. Quick, Mom, quick!"

11

They drove down streets Kix had never seen before, scanning the sides of the road for animals and peering between rows of trees and into fields, yards, and gardens. Kix had brought the binoculars with him, but they weren't really much help. You only saw one strip, one slice of town.

"You face backward, and I'll look forward," Kix told Emilia, because then they'd see twice as much.

Mom drove as slow as she could, and now and then Emilia shouted, "Switch!" or "Stop!" That meant she'd seen a flash of something, a blur of white or maybe brown. "Sam!" she'd call out, or "Choca!"

But they were always the wrong dogs, or sometimes even cats, way too small, way too thin, and a few times Kix felt like hitting his sister again.

They stopped at the copy center, where Mom got the poster she'd made on the computer enlarged and printed. Two hundred copies. They carried a big pile of them back out to the car. It had taken ages, and all that time Kix had thought that they'd be better off driving around. Soon it would start to get dark, and he was still convinced they would see Sam — if they managed to find Choca.

"We have to search the next town too," Kix said when they were finally back in Mom's SUV.

Mom hesitated.

"We can hang those posters up tomorrow," Kix said. He pronounced the words forcefully. He had to if he wanted his mother to listen.

"Alright," she said. "One more hour. That's all."

They were driving down a country road way out on the other side of the next town. "We're going back," Mom said. "We've gone way too far, and it will be dark in ten minutes."

"It won't get really dark," said Kix. "Not with all this snow. Just a bit longer."

"Please," Emilia said, "just a little bit longer. We don't have a plane, so we have to make do with the car."

In the last hour they hadn't even had any arguments. Emilia was helping really well, searching just as carefully as Kix. And maybe she had the best eyes, because suddenly she shouted, "Choca! There! And this time I'm right!"

Kix had almost given up hoping, but his mother leaned over the steering wheel, peering through the windshield.

"Where?"

"There!" Emilia pointed.

Kix grabbed his binoculars. He could see something dark, a dog on a long chain at the back of a big farm, and he shouted, "I think it might be her, Mom. Stop!"

They turned into the driveway. There were lights on in the windows of the house, and there, in their headlights, right in front of the car, was Choca. It was really her!

Kix and Emilia jumped out into the snow. They ran up to Choca and looked around — was Sam there too? No, not yet. They raced back to their mother, who was standing at the front door of the house talking to a woman.

Kix's heart was going *kaboom-kaboom* everywhere: in his chest, in his throat, even in his ears.

Mom showed the lady one of the posters. She told her about Choca visiting Sam, and asked if maybe he . . .

"Yes," said the lady, "I recognize him alright. That's a beautiful dog. And he was here. Not long ago . . . the day before yesterday, maybe? Or the day before that? But he didn't stay long. And since then . . ."

Now Kix's heart wasn't making any sound at all. It had just stopped beating.

" . . . Since then we haven't seen him at all."

12

It was a quiet drive home. Kix had a strange taste in his mouth and didn't like it. Now and then his mother said things like, "We'll find him," and "Maybe he's already on his way back home after visiting Choca," and "Tomorrow we'll hang the posters up all over town. Everywhere, Kix, you hear me?" It was meant to cheer him up, but it didn't work.

And when they were almost home, things got even worse.

They were just about to turn into their driveway when the neighbor from across the road appeared. He walked out of the gloom and waved at Mom.

She stopped and got out of the car.

Kix opened his window so he could hear what they were saying.

Mr. Jones and his wife were old and grumpy, but since the summer they'd been a lot friendlier to him than they were before.

Flint, who used to be Sam's owner, was their son. And Kix had experienced the scariest night of his life with him. It had turned out well in the end, but it wasn't something he liked to think back on.

What did Mr. Jones want? Did he have some news about Flint? Or, or — had he found Sam?

No, he'd found Springer.

They had let her escape — Mom, Emilia, and Kix. They hadn't been paying attention earlier when they'd driven off. That was stupid of them, and hopefully Dad wouldn't find out. Mr. Jones had looked after Springer, who had come galloping onto his lawn. He'd put her on a leash.

Kix slumped back in his seat. It was Springer who'd been found, not Sam. That was all they had to show for their day's work. He listened to his mother telling Mr. Jones about their failed search for Sam — but then their neighbor whistled.

He whistled through his teeth, and it was an ominous sound.

"I hope for your sake," he told Mom, "that your dog didn't wander too close to the feedlot. They don't like loose dogs over there. Last week the guys working there blew two of them away. Two strays. They'd gone after the feed, of course. Saint Bernards. Nice-looking dogs. I've seen 'em around here sometimes. Bang, bang, dead."

When Mr. Jones said, "Bang, bang, dead," it was like two guns going off inside Kix.

Tom and Jerry were dead.

The two magnificent Saint Bernards who had been to visit in the horse pasture just a couple of weeks ago had gotten too close to the feedlot.

The men who worked at the feedlot were hard. Kix knew that. And they had guns too. Farmers sent them their pigs and cows to fatten them up before turning them into chops and sausages. That's why there was plenty of feed at the feedlot. It attracted hungry strays, and the men shot them.

Before, during, and after supper, Kix couldn't think about anything else. He poked at his macaroni, then slid away his plate.

Dad said Mr. Jones was an old blabbermouth. Mom said that Kix should never have opened the car window. But the bitter taste in Kix's mouth had gotten worse. He couldn't help it — he was thinking about that night with Flint.

That was when Flint was loony. Mom said Kix shouldn't call people that. But that night when Kix had crept through the dark by himself to the Jones's farm to free Sam, Flint was standing there. And his eyes had had a wild glow in them. And he had a gun too.

Kix had managed to calm Flint down. But then Kix's

dad had showed up, an argument started, and in the end it was Kix who went to stand between the two gun-toting men. He was scared all the way down to the soles of his feet, but he didn't stop to think.

But now real shots had been fired, and they'd hit their targets: a hole in the head of one Saint Bernard and then a hole in the head of the other one and maybe even in —

Kix let out a sob. Just for a second, a quiet whimper that slipped out of his throat, but everyone heard it. And something dripped down onto the edge of his plate, coming from his eyes.

Emilia slid her chair closer. She put an arm around his shoulders.

But Dad stood up.

He walked over to the coatrack and took down his coat, and Kix's too.

"Come on," he said. "We're going to the feedlot."

This time Kix didn't open his window. He didn't listen in. He couldn't anyway, because the engine of the car was still running, and his father was twenty or thirty feet away.

Cold steam was puffing out of Dad's mouth, and out of the feedlot man's mouth too. A streetlight was shining down on them.

Kix saw the feedlot guy shake his head. He saw him shrug. He saw him raise his hands as if to say he had nothing to do with it.

He saw Dad nod. He watched the last little clouds hang in the air, one from the man and one from Dad — and then his father stalked back to the car.

The door opened.

Cold air rushed in.

The door slammed shut again.

"Well," Dad said, "he hasn't been here. They didn't shoot any white dogs."

"But Tom and Jerry?"

Dad swore. "They're bastards, those guys. Bastards. But at least our Sam really hasn't been here."

That helped. A bit.

But Kix didn't want to be read to that night either. Of course he didn't.

He couldn't get Tom and Jerry out of his head, and he knew it was going to take him a long time to fall asleep.

Emilia snuck into his room. She came when it was already late, and Dad and Mom were watching a movie across the hall.

She stood next to his bed, fidgeted with the hem of her pajama top, and said, "Sam wouldn't really go to a feedlot. He doesn't even like food. He likes being petted. And I don't think they do that at feedlots."

Kix laughed for a moment. And then new tears welled up in his eyes.

But it did help. A little bit.

13

Since Mom didn't have to teach any music classes the next day, she hung up posters everywhere. Sam's faithful face stared out at people from all the store windows and caught their eye from all of the lampposts.

When Mom picked up Kix and Emilia from school, they saw it for themselves.

On Saturday Kix had a hockey game. He scored, even though he couldn't stop thinking about Sam. His classmates knew what had happened, and so did his teammates. Maybe they gave him an easy shot on purpose, so he only needed to swing his stick and *wham* — into the goal. To give him something happy to think about.

Kix walked through the fields one more time with his dad. His mother called the shelter and the local animal hospitals. Grandma and Grandpa drove to nearby towns they hadn't searched yet.

But nobody found Sam.

People who had seen the posters thought they recognized Sam and called their number, but when Mom and Kix jumped in the car to go take a look, the dogs they pointed out were beautiful, and sometimes even mountain dogs, but never Sam.

Days passed, and then it had been a whole week.

Two whole weeks.

Mom, Dad, Grandma, Grandpa — everyone kept saying that Sam would come back. "He decides for himself when and where to stay," they said. "Soon he'll be back out there wagging his tail as if nothing ever happened."

And one night Kix dreamed that he'd been woken up by a slurping noise — the sound Sam made when he was drinking from a puddle, with his big red tongue hanging out of his mouth. But it was a sound in a dream. Then Kix really did wake up, and he heard only the silence, broken now and then by a train's whistle. And no answer from Sam.

What's more, it was still winter, and there was a thick layer of ice on all the puddles.

A few days after that, Kix caught his mother crying.

Emilia had gone to Grandpa's with Dad. Kix had been at the campground with his friends, but they'd been picked up early.

When Kix got back home, he heard loud music: Mom was playing a sad song.

Kix stood in the doorway listening. It was coming from the computer. There was a video to go with it of a cartoon cat singing a farewell song for a dog. It was called "So Long, Old Friend."

Kix took a step toward the couch. Mom thought she was alone — she hadn't heard him come in. And she was crying.

For a moment Kix wobbled on his feet. He didn't know whether to tiptoe back out or go further into the room. But then the song finished. Mom wiped her eyes and got up to go over to the computer. She saw Kix and said, "Oh."

"Mom," Kix said, "what are you doing?"

Mom sat down again and patted the couch. "Come here for a second."

Kix didn't know if that was something he wanted to do. He slowly took off his coat, and then even more slowly walked in the other direction. Not far, just to a chair at the kitchen table. He hung his coat over the back of the chair. Then he turned around after all and shuffled back to the living room.

The couch cushions sighed as he sat down, and Kix sighed too.

"I think . . ." Mom said, talking straight ahead to herself but with words that were meant for Kix, "I think we made a mistake. We should have called the vet much sooner. Because now we have to get used to the idea that Sam's not

coming back. It's been almost three weeks now, and we haven't been able to find him anywhere. We can only believe that he's wandered off. And that he was sick, I think. Sam would never have gone away if he was healthy. And we have to be grateful that he was with us. We have to remember the beautiful times we . . ."

"MOM!" Kix screamed. He covered his ears with his hands and shouted, "Could you please stop it?"

He ran, still deaf, to the kitchen chair, to his coat, lowered his arms for a moment to stick them into the sleeves, then pressed his hands against his ears again — and then he was gone. Out of the kitchen, out of the laundry room, through the garage, and outside.

He was panting a little. He blinked in the low sunlight and took his hands off his ears. The whole world was still hidden under snow. Out here nobody was talking about Sam being sick and unhealthy and wandering around somewhere in pain until he . . .

Kix walked over to the stable. He hadn't dared to go in since Sam left, because he didn't want to see Sam's cushion and Sam's food bowl. But now he knew what he was looking for.

He found it too, right away. Sam's brush. With hair bulging out of the bristles, clouds of white hair.

Kix pressed his nose against it, and for a moment Sam was back. He hadn't disappeared at all. Not Sam.

14

His mother didn't bring it up again.

That evening Kix asked her if she could read some more *Bunnicula*. The funny chapter about Chester the cat hanging garlic up all over the house, because garlic doesn't just work against vampires, but against vampire rabbits too.

Kix laughed, because fortunately there wasn't anything at all about lost dogs in *Bunnicula*.

But as soon as Kix was alone again, the questions came back. If Sam went looking for Choca, why didn't he stay with her? Was Sam sick? Or had he had enough of their farm and their family? Had they done something wrong? Had Sam found other kids to live with? Were they ruffling his hair and rubbing their faces against his coat now? Had Sam followed the trains perhaps? Or gone after a pack of coyotes? Or was Mom right and was he . . .

Kix hit himself. Slap, on the forehead. He'd rather feel pain than imagine answers to the questions that were worrying him.

Last week, after hockey practice, Kix had punched a boy in the face. Hard. The coach probably hadn't told Mom, because he hadn't punished Kix for it either. The other kid had deserved it. He'd only just started hockey, and he couldn't really skate properly, and he'd laughed at Kix's stories about Sam. From the other side of the locker room he'd said, "That dog's been buried under the snow for ages." That was when Kix had run at him.

At night, after bedtime, Kix was like his little sister. He got strange thoughts in his head, just as strange as hers sometimes, and he couldn't help it.

Like really wanting to rent a plane, or a helicopter. They could fly low over the towns, and Kix could look down through a hole in the floor and see all the animals wandering around the fields.

Or else he'd imagine that somebody had glued a transmitter to the inside of Sam's ear. Then all you'd need would be a receiver, and you'd see a red dot on the screen, and that would be Sam.

Even better: one day Kix would go outside, and there'd be a cloud hanging over their yard. A cloud in the shape of an arrow. They'd follow it in the car, and eventually the arrow would point at a white animal, a white animal from a land of mystery.

They were Emilia-like thoughts, and Kix never mentioned them, but in the meantime Emilia herself was coming up with new plans too.

On Monday, after the fourth weekend since Sam had disappeared, she told her friends that they all had to go outside after they got home from school and spend an hour calling, "Sam! Sam! Sam!"

Did they do it? Kix didn't hear another word about it later, but at least Emilia thought that Sam was still alive.

That cheered him up. Because Sam *was* still alive! Kix really didn't want to believe it could be any other way.

But sometimes it was difficult, because Mom and Dad didn't agree with him. Kix could feel it. He'd looked up the song Mom had played on YouTube. It was a farewell song — you wouldn't play it unless you were sure you'd never see someone again.

Grandpa came over for supper again, like he did every Thursday. This time he didn't say much about Sam, but he did mention that a farmer he visited every now and then had found some white hair on an old mattress in the corner of his yard.

"From Sam!" cried Emilia, and Kix asked him where the farmer lived.

"Pretty far from here," said Grandpa. He added that he'd driven around that farmer's fields right away. But no, nothing.

That was one word Kix was really getting sick of. *Nothing.*

A few more days passed, and Kix had almost stopped looking left and right over the yard when he went outside.

He'd almost given up.

Almost.

15

Aunt Julie and her chatterbox daughters were coming to stay during spring break. Emilia got along really well with all three of them and was planning lots of doll parties and craft projects.

Mom had to laugh at Emilia's ideas, but she was looking forward to spending lots of time sitting at the kitchen table with Aunt Julie, who was her sister. Dad wouldn't be around: he built houses, and now he had to go to the far side of the province for a few days to put up a barn.

And Kix got to go with Grandpa to his cabin in the mountains.

The cabin was right at the very start of the mountains, at the beginning of the foothills. Kix liked to think of the mountain range as an enormous giant, with Grandma and Grandpa's little wooden cabin perched on his toes.

It was fantastic for sledding in winter and rolling down the hills in summer. There was a lake they'd dammed themselves, with a landing and a ladder, and when Kix and Emilia slept in the spare room they had a view out over the tops of the pine trees growing further down the hill. The treetops were always swaying gently back and forth, even when there wasn't any wind.

And now Kix got to go there by himself. He'd bake pies

with Grandma, who was already there and bound to have the kitchen smelling sweet already, and maybe he would ride around the lake on the snowmobile with Grandpa.

But first they had to drive an hour and a half in the Chevy, with a stop halfway at Tim Hortons for an enormous hot chocolate.

Grandpa had the deepest voice Kix had ever heard. Grandpa was strong, and he usually called Kix "buddy," so they were basically friends.

And friends don't keep secrets from each other.

Friends talk about everything.

That's why Kix was upset by what he had accidentally overheard, just as they were about to leave.

He was standing at the back door of Grandpa's car. Mom and Grandpa must have forgotten he was there for a moment, because his mother said, "Dad, he's still not himself."

"Who?" Grandpa asked. "Kix?"

"He still thinks Sam's going to turn up at the door one day."

"What's wrong with that, honey? He can keep hoping, can't he?"

"Yes, but, Dad . . ." And now Mom started whispering, but Kix could still hear what she was saying. " Sometimes I think we need to tell him that . . ."

"Oh?" said Grandpa. "You haven't talked to him yet?"

"I didn't want to upset him."

"Sarah, he's nine years old. He can cope with the truth."

"I know. But we don't need to assume that . . . either way, Dad, don't say too much to him . . ."

Kix took a stiff-legged step backward. He didn't move

when Mom hugged him a little later, and he was still stiff when he climbed into the car.

"Wave goodbye," said Grandpa. And Kix did, with a wooden hand he could hardly lift.

16

The day had turned gray, but the air in Grandpa's car was even darker.

Kix was allowed to sit in the front, and Grandpa put on country music. Grandpa loved country music.

But not Kix. Not today. They were just outside of town, Grandpa was humming along, and suddenly Kix couldn't take it anymore. He turned the volume down.

Grandpa didn't say anything. He just looked over at Kix for a moment. He hummed a few more lines, then went quiet.

A little while later, he said, "Not easy, is it?"

Kix didn't know what to say to that.

"I mean," said Grandpa, "being with somebody who's in a good mood when you're not."

Kix still didn't know what to say.

"Listen, buddy," Grandpa said, "if you want to curse or swear about your dog, that's fine by me. We're far enough away from your parents, and I don't see any churches near here either."

Kix didn't want to swear. That wouldn't make the inky air in the car any lighter. But he did kick. He kicked the bottom of Grandpa's new dashboard.

"Okay," Grandpa said. "Just make sure you don't activate

the airbag. Those things expand real fast. Before you know it, you'll have yourself a broken arm."

Kix kicked the dashboard again.

"Sure," said Grandpa. "Let me know when I can put the music back on."

And then Kix exploded. "Never! I don't want any music again! Ever!"

Grandpa raised one arm and was about to say "okay" again, but he didn't get a chance, because Kix kept shouting, "Never ever! And you were just lying to me! You and Mom and Dad and everyone, and it doesn't matter anyway. IT DOESN'T MATTER BECAUSE I'VE KNOWN THE TRUTH FOR AGES!"

Tears had rushed to his eyes, but his voice was still clear. His words came out as a scream. "I'VE KNOWN IT ALL ALONG!"

Grandpa didn't say anything. He reached out to Kix, took hold of his shoulder, and squeezed it. It didn't hurt, but Kix still gasped and shouted, "OW! DAMN IT, GRANDPA, OW!"

Now he'd sworn after all. Kix was a bit shocked.

But not Grandpa.

Grandpa said very softly, "What do you know, Kix? What truth are you talking about exactly?"

And then Kix had to say it — the most horrible thing in the world — out loud: "Sam is dead."

Right away Grandpa slammed on the brakes. The car swerved to the side, and it was a good thing the road was deserted because they skidded to a halt with two wheels on the road and two on the shoulder.

Grandpa unbuckled his seatbelt, turned to face Kix,

and said, "That's not the truth, Kix. You hear me? It doesn't need to be the truth!"

"No?" Kix shouted. "You were standing there talking with Mom, both of you! SAM IS DEAD! HE'S BEEN BURIED UNDER THE SNOW SOMEWHERE FOR AGES!"

"Get out," Grandpa said.

What? Suddenly Kix didn't need to scream anymore. What had Grandpa said?

"Get out," Grandpa repeated. He sounded strict. "Walk around the car and open my door."

Kix didn't know what was happening. Was he being punished? He stared at Grandpa's face, but Grandpa just gestured at the handle under Kix's window.

Kix stared at the handle. But then he pushed it down, opened the car door, and jumped out. It was cold, and he wasn't wearing a coat. Did Grandpa know that — that it was so cold?

Kix walked past the hood of the Chevy. He looked at the windshield, which was reflecting the sky. He hesitated for a moment, then kept walking.

Once he'd walked around the car, Grandpa's door flew open.

"Come here," said Grandpa.

Kix stepped forward and suddenly felt Grandpa's strong arms around him, pulling him up. Grandpa had slid his seat back, and suddenly Kix was sitting on his lap.

The car door slammed shut, and before Kix really understood what had happened, Grandpa began to whisper: "Buddy, listen. Your mother's just worried. About you. She wants to be gentle with you. She's not keeping anything secret from you, but I did keep something secret from you. And I'm not going to do that anymore, because you have

60

a right to know what I'm thinking. About Sam, I mean. I don't know if it's the truth, but I'm afraid it probably is."

It was quiet for a moment in the car. Kix was still trying to get used to the situation having changed so quickly — to being able to feel Grandpa's legs under his own. To hearing Grandpa's voice, deep and with a few little cracks in it, just an inch or two away from his ears.

But Grandpa had started talking again. "Sam is old. You know that. And when dogs get old, especially big dogs, they suffer ailments. Sam's worked hard his whole life, in every season and all kinds of weather. That wears a dog out. They get creaky bones, and sometimes their joints start to ache. They're no different from people like that. But . . ."

Grandpa took a deep breath and moved his legs a little so Kix could get more comfortable. "But it's not just their bodies that wear out. Their heads do too. Just like some old people. Except it's more common with dogs, especially big dogs. As they get older, their memory starts to fail. Their brains don't work as well. They get confused. They forget where their food bowl is, things like that. So I think . . ."

"No," said Kix. "No, Grandpa, that's not right. Sam's not like that. Sam's smart, and he knows where his food bowl is, really, he does."

"Buddy," Grandpa said, "believe me, I've seen it before. Some days there's nothing wrong. They wake up, and they're completely themselves, wise and friendly from living a long life. But on other days, they've lost their way. That's usually how you notice. They lie down in the strangest places. They don't know anymore whether they want to go inside or out, and then they stand there staring at a door or lie down on the step for hours. They whimper more often. They seem distracted and dreamy.

61

"Maybe you don't believe me, maybe you'll be angry at me the whole time you're at the cabin, but it's like this — I think Sam's been a bit forgetful for a while now. And I'm guessing that he wandered off on one of those confused days, and couldn't remember which direction he'd gone or which route he'd taken, and then he couldn't find his way back home.

"Just think about it, buddy. Think about these last few months. The way Sam's been acting, all those mornings he was vague and drowsy. If you want the truth, that's what I think the truth is.

"And now I'm going to put you back in your seat. We'll keep driving, and we won't say anything else. You think about it, and if you want to kick my dashboard, I think it's a shame, for the dash, I mean, but if that's the way it has to be, that's the way it has to be."

17

It wasn't true. It couldn't be. How could his dog, who had scared off a pack of coyotes with two barks, really be a forgetful old man?

In the first few minutes after Grandpa started driving again, Kix still felt like kicking something. Or smashing one of the windows of Grandpa's stupid new Chevy.

But he didn't.

Because suddenly he saw it:

Sam lying down in the middle of the road,

Sam standing at the garage door,

Sam almost getting stuck in the back corner of the stable,

Sam whimpering more and more often and sounding sadder and sadder,

and above all, how blank his expression could be sometimes. How his thoughts seemed to be somewhere else, or maybe *nowhere else*.

Kix was still angry. He still wanted to kick things and swear at the top of his lungs, but at the same time, he realized now that Grandpa and Mom and Dad didn't think Sam was dead. They thought he was lost!

Kix looked out the window. That way he didn't have to see Grandpa's eyes.

Not that Grandpa was looking at him, not even close — he was just staring at the road, maybe already thinking about what Grandma would make for supper tonight.

Or maybe not.

Grandpa knew a lot about dogs.

But did he also know a lot about what goes on inside a dog's head?

It wasn't until they stopped for hot chocolate that Kix knew what to say. And to his surprise, it didn't even come out angry. "Grandpa," he said, "I don't think it's true what you said, because maybe Sam was a bit confused sometimes, but most of the time he wasn't. And he wanted to play all the time. I'm not making it up. You weren't around then, but he'd always go to the campground with me. And then he was young again. And someone who's young can't be so old that his brain doesn't work anymore."

They were sitting opposite each other at a window table. It took a while for Grandpa to answer. He looked at Kix, blew on his coffee, and said, "Dementia."

"What?"

"It's like a second puppyhood," Grandpa said. "That's another way of putting it. Look, I don't want to make things even worse, but that's what can happen with old dogs. Like old people, they go through a second childhood. The old memories are stronger than the new ones. It's like they go back to when they were little. They get more playful. More puppyish. They forget what they just experienced, but remember everything from the old days. And that shows in the way they act. Dementia. That's what it's called."

Grandpa took a mouthful of coffee. But this time he'd forgotten to blow on it and burned his tongue. Kix saw it happen.

"Sorry," said Grandpa.

"You burned your tongue," said Kix.

"No, not because of that," Grandpa said. "Sorry for having to tell you all this. About Sam."

Kix didn't answer.

And going back out into the cold and climbing into the car and looking ahead through the windshield with Grandpa — it had started snowing again — he didn't say anything either.

He was thinking. Everything Grandpa had said swirled in his head with all the things that had happened in the last few months.

It calmed him down, though he didn't understand why.

And they'd driven on for maybe half an hour when it suddenly became clear to him. Kix didn't need to kick anything or make a racket, because all at once he heard himself saying, "Grandpa, I know where he is. I know where Sam is."

18

Grandpa didn't react right away.

He didn't hit the brakes, either, and he didn't pull over to the side of the road. He just waited a few more minutes.

Kix didn't mind. He waited a few minutes too, then said again, "I know where Sam went. I should have thought of it before."

"We're almost home," said Grandpa.

"Uh-huh," said Kix.

"So where do you think he is?" Grandpa asked.

"Home," said Kix. "Sam's gone home too. To his old home, I mean. He's gone looking for the farm where he worked. Where he used to live. Where he guarded the sheep. If what you said is true, about puppyhood and all that, then that's where he's gone. I'm sure of it."

Grandpa looked at Kix. He raised his eyebrows slightly, then lowered them again. He took one hand off the steering wheel and scratched his cheek.

"Buddy . . ." he said, "do you really think so?"

And then Kix did what Grandpa had done to him earlier that afternoon. He laid a hand on Grandpa's shoulder. He gave it a little squeeze and said, "Yes."

"Buddy," said Grandpa again, whacking the steering wheel with his hand, "that means he's gone looking for a farm that's been sold . . . that no longer exists. The farm he lived on with . . ."

"Yes," Kix said. "With Flint."

19

Grandma and Grandpa's cabin was right in front of them. Kix saw smoke rising from the chimney and steam coming from a vent near the kitchen. That meant Grandma was baking, just as he'd expected. But he didn't do what he would have done otherwise — run in and leap into Grandma's arms — because he was thinking about Flint. And Flint's old farm.

Grandpa walked alongside him in the gently falling snow. They stepped up onto the porch, but Grandpa wasn't thinking about Grandma either.

"It won't be easy, buddy," he said. "That farm probably belongs to someone else now. Or else it's empty. I know Flint. He's not actually a bad guy. Before he cracked up, of course. But that farm of his — he made a mess of it. The land's probably sold by now. If Sam managed to make his way back, then . . . well, whatever else, he won't have come back to the place he knew before."

They stayed standing by the front door. Grandpa put his hand on the door handle, but Kix said, "Is it far? That farm was somewhere in the foothills too, wasn't it? Is it far from here?"

The door opened, and there was Grandma. "Boys! You going to stay outside all night?"

"Hi there," Grandpa said, but then immediately turned

back to Kix. "Not really," he said. "It's not far. Not even half an hour. I helped him with a horse every now and then."

"Grandpa!" Kix shouted, and Grandma gave them both a strange look. "Grandpa! We have to go there right now!"

Yes, they had to go and look for Sam. It couldn't wait. Kix wolfed down his hamburger. He was in a hurry — he didn't need any dessert. "Come on," he wanted to scream. "Now!"

Sam, Sam, Sam, sounded in his head.

But Grandpa thought they needed to eat calmly, and now he was telling the whole story to Grandma. It took ages, and when he was finished he even said, "Yeah, I don't know . . ."

But then Grandma put her foot down. "What do you mean, you don't know? What if the boy's right?"

Kix jumped up and grabbed his coat. Of course he was right.

But Grandpa hadn't stopped mumbling. Now he was talking about how late it was. And that it was dark. And snowing. And that they could go tomorrow morning . . .

"No!" said Kix.

"Oh," said Grandma, looking at the clock. "It *is* already past seven."

Kix stomped over to her. "We have to do it now! We can go and look for Sam because now we know where he is. And if we don't do it now, we're not worth a dime."

Grandma laughed for a moment, and so did Grandpa. "Not worth a dime," he said. "No, we don't want to be that."

"Come on then, Grandpa!" Kix cried. "And you too, Grandma!"

"Kix . . ." said Grandma.

Sam's name started to pound through his head again. *Sam, Sam, Sam.*

"Wait!" Kix said. He just managed to avoid shouting in Grandpa's ear. "Mom sent a video. To you, Grandpa, a while ago, on your cell phone! Have you still got it? Where's your phone?"

Grandpa's phone was in the living room. And when they'd finally found the video, they saw Sam. At the campground, rolling on his back and sneezing in the snow.

"Like a puppy, Grandpa!" Kix shouted. "Here's proof!"

He kicked a table leg, because why were they still . . .

"What do you mean, like a puppy?" Grandma asked, but she didn't wait for an answer. She told Grandpa, "Look at that dog. And look at your grandson. Get a move on, you're going. Just take a look — you can do that. It's not far. What if he *is* there?"

And with that, it was decided.

They went.

20

It was crackly cold, but the wind was holding off, and the snowflakes were falling straight down as if they were leaking out of the sky.

Kix stared through the dark windshield. White on black was all that he could see, with yellow headlight beams at the bottom.

Next to him, Grandpa was talking. "We're just going to take a quick look. Don't get your hopes up."

Kix didn't respond. He was trying to catch a message from his dog. It was too early still for Sam's night howl, but wasn't that a very quiet *Kix! Here!* he was hearing? A kind of murmur in the distance. In between Grandpa's words, almost drowned out by the noise of the Chevy. He should really open the window and . . .

"Kix?" said Grandpa. "Buddy?"

Kix looked over at him. He gave his head a brief shake so he could pay attention to what Grandpa was going to say.

"Prepare yourself."

"What?"

"Prepare yourself for a disappointment. I want you to be ready for . . ."

"Are we already there?" Kix didn't need to hear the end of Grandpa's sentence. "Is it here somewhere?"

Grandpa didn't reply. He wasn't looking strict or stern, but he did look serious.

"Okay," he said, "you heard me."

And then he put his turn signal on, steered to the left, and said, "It's at the end of this road."

21

The farm was on a hill. The road leading up to it was narrow, and they had to get out to pry open a gate. After that there was another road, and that one seemed to go on forever too.

Finally they stopped.

Grandpa turned off the engine, and the lights went off. "This is it," he said.

Kix tried to peer through the dim moonlight. And to listen. Both.

"Coat zipped up tight? Cap on snug?" asked Grandpa.

They got out.

They slammed the car doors. Two thumps with slight echoes.

"By the looks of things," Grandpa said, "there aren't any new owners. I guess the bank hasn't been able to sell it yet."

It had stopped snowing, and it was so clear and quiet that Kix could hear his own breathing, and his heart.

"Sam?" he said quietly. It was the kind of place that made you start whispering.

Grandpa clicked on his flashlight and shone it over the yard. Now Kix could see the farm.

This was where Sam had grown up. Where he had worked. And now he was hiding out here.

Hopefully. Probably.

A snowy field stretched away on their left, maybe with a pasture buried underneath. There were pine trees around it, just like at Grandma and Grandpa's cabin. The branches were drooping, weighed down by heavy white loads.

"Sam?" Kix whispered again.

On their right was the house. It wasn't big, but the boarded-up windows made it look like a giant black monster.

"Grandpa," said Kix, still whispering, "we have to look under it."

One side of the monster house was on the top of the hill, and the other side stood on thick legs. To reach the front door, you had to climb up steps to the porch. The porch ran all the way round the house, but there were posts under it, and deeper in the darkness, Kix could see a basement, or maybe a storage room. A perfect hiding place for an outdoor dog who liked to stay close to people.

Grandpa shone his flashlight over the house and took a few steps toward it. Kix ran on ahead as best he could through the deep snow.

He reached the stairs and crouched down.

He heard Grandpa say, "Wait a sec."

But Kix was already moving in under the porch with his head down. "Sam?" he said. "Sam?"

If his dog was here, Kix's voice would draw him out of the shadows. That was what would happen, *that was what would happen*! But nothing moved at the front of the house. There was a lot of junk lying there: a bucket, some loose tiles, a few logs.

Around the side then. "Sam? Sam?"

Grandpa's light followed Kix around. Now the back of the house.

Nothing.

The other side?

No.

Kix was back at the steps.

"He's not here," Kix said.

Suddenly he could picture Sam — dirty and exhausted after walking for weeks with aching knees. And then nobody living here.

"Or . . ." Kix said, and he could hear his heart again, "or he's not here any*more*!"

"Come on," said Grandpa. "This is just the house. We'll check the barns and sheds."

Of course! The stable and the sheep shed! Grandpa turned down a path Kix hadn't even noticed. They only had to take half a dozen steps, and suddenly they could see a yard that was at least five times as big as the yard at Kix's house. "Wow," he said. "Wow . . ."

"Yep," said Grandpa, "Flint was doing pretty well in the beginning. It's not a ranch, I wouldn't go that far, but he had a nice operation here for a one-man band."

"Sam's in one of those sheds!" Kix shouted. And he started to run, half-lit by Grandpa's flashlight and half-lit by the light from the moon and the snow.

The first barn was the smallest. The door was locked, and even sealed, but you could walk all the way around it.

Kix could see that there was no way Sam could have gotten inside, but he still knocked on the wooden walls. He pressed his ear against them. Could he hear something? "Sam? Sam? You in there?"

After the fourth barn, that ear had turned to ice.

Together with Grandpa, Kix had listened at all the

doors and checked all the locks, and when that hadn't gotten them anywhere, they'd gone to have a look between a bunch of bare trees, and in an open shed, and in a field.

"Kix . . ." Grandpa said.

Kix didn't say anything. He looked around. Maybe there was another field?

"Kix," Grandpa said again. "Kix."

"Are there any neighbors?" Kix asked. "Maybe he went to the wrong house."

"Buddy," Grandpa said. "We should have found some tracks by now. Or tufts of hair."

"They would have blown away!" Kix swung his arms around, mimicking a chinook.

"Son . . ." Grandpa said. He switched off the flashlight, and suddenly they were standing very still in the darkness.

But Kix wasn't planning on giving up. "We can't stop now," he whispered. "What's down there?"

He walked back to the car, back to the pines in front of the house.

He asked Grandpa to switch the flashlight back on and shine it across the row of trees. Wasn't that a path he could see?

"Grandpa!" he yelled. "This way! Here!"

He started running across the yard. The snow flew up, and Kix just managed to keep from slipping. There really was a path. It led down the hill, away from the house. Kix peered through the pine trees.

He called out, "Bring the flashlight over here!"

But he didn't need it anymore. Kix stopped breathing. He pushed a thick branch out of the way. It dropped its layer of snow and shot up, freed from its burden, and now

Kix could see what was there, just a little further along the path, not that far down the hill.

A cabin.

A cabin that belonged to the farm.

There was a car next to it. And while Grandpa came panting up next to him, Kix stared at the cabin windows.

There was a light on, and someone was moving around inside. That person stood up to grab something or set something down on a table.

"Grandpa," said Kix, "look."

"Dang," said Grandpa. "If it's not Flint."

22

Flint still had a crack in his voice. His beard was still black. And he still had the same eyes. They were small and dark. Kix had gotten a good look at them once, on the scariest night of his life.

The two of them had faced off that night. Flint with a gun, and Kix with nothing. At first Flint might have been planning to shoot Sam dead. But then Kix had shouted that Sam was the boss and that Sam got to choose. And then, in the nick of time, Flint's fierce black eyes had calmed down a little and started looking more like normal eyes.

And now Kix recognized them: Flint's eyes in Flint's face. They seemed to have calmed down even more and gotten even more normal. Flint wasn't sick anymore. And it wasn't really scary to sit down now at a table with him. And with Grandpa.

"No," Flint said, "I haven't seen him."

Grandpa told him about Sam. Flint had grabbed a couple of cans of beer for Grandpa and himself. And water for Kix, since he didn't have anything else.

Flint leaned back and took a cigarette from the pack on the counter.

"I haven't seen him," he repeated, "but I only just got here myself."

Kix took a small sip of water. He watched Flint snap a flame to life with his lighter. He'd done that back then too, on that night.

"Oh?" Grandpa asked. "You going to start it up again? Your farm?"

"No idea," Flint said. He pursed his lips to stop the smoke from his mouth from blowing straight over the table. "I'm broke. But the bank doesn't have any buyers for the farm either. The deal is that I keep an eye on things. And in exchange I'm living here now. This cabin was always for visitors and . . ."

Kix had been shy for a while. But now he couldn't keep it in any longer. He jumped up. "Stop it!" he shouted. "Stop yakking!"

It was immediately quiet.

"Kix," Grandpa said calmly. "Do you know what time it is? We've tried everything. I knew coming here was a risk. We haven't found Sam, and now you're upset."

Grandpa was almost whispering.

"Come here for a moment," he said. He patted his thighs. He meant for Kix to come over and sit on his lap. "Tomorrow we can ask around the area. And if Flint sees our dog, he'll be sure to —"

"I'm not upset!" Kix said. "But . . . it's just . . ."

He was sure Sam had to be somewhere close by. There could only be one thing Sam longed for more than staying with Kix, Emilia, Springer, and all of them — and that was his old life. If Sam had forgotten the things he was experiencing in the present and only remembered the old days, he'd want to go back to the sheep and horses he'd watched over. How could Sam understand that they were all gone? They were still there inside his head.

Of course he'd gone looking for them, back in time, back into his memories. Kix had never been so sure of anything. But Grandpa didn't understand. Not anymore.

"Grandpa," Kix cried, "why don't you understand anymore?"

Now Grandpa looked shocked. He stood up and reached out to Kix with one hand. But Kix took a step back. All of a sudden he'd had a thought that was so new and so serious and scary he didn't know if he should say it out loud.

He looked to the side for a moment, at Flint. He wasn't moving. The cigarette between his fingers was burning all by itself.

Kix made a decision.

He turned back to Grandpa and said, "If we don't go looking now, it will be my fault."

Grandpa wanted to answer, but Kix wasn't finished yet. "I know Sam is here. I understand him. Sometimes he talks to me. Sometimes he whimpers, but then he's actually saying sorry, or telling me what happened. It's been like that for ages, and I'm the only one who understands him. But we haven't found him yet, and that means something's happened. He's old, Grandpa, you said so yourself. And if something goes wrong tonight, then . . ."

Kix had betrayed him. All this time Sam's messages had been his secret. But the tingling goosebumps on Kix's arms weren't from betraying someone. They were from the thought he had to say out loud. "Grandpa, if we go home and Sam dies tonight . . ."

Kix took a deep breath.

" . . . then we killed him."

It was warm in Flint's kitchen, which also doubled as his living room. There was a woodstove burning in the corner. But there was a layer of ice on Kix's arms. Because of what he'd said.

Grandpa and Flint were still staring at Kix, and Kix stared back.

They didn't know what to do next.

But Flint was flapping his hand in the air. The cigarette had burned his finger. He slid back his chair, walked over to the faucet, and held his hand under the stream.

Grandpa coughed. "No —" he began, but he didn't get further than that single word, because he was interrupted by his coat. It flew into his chest. Flint had grabbed it off a chair and thrown it at Grandpa. *Zoofff*, followed by Kix's.

"Get a move on," Flint said, striding off.

"And call your wife!" he shouted back at Grandpa from the hall. "We'll go down past the sheep pasture and, if we have to, into the woods. We'll search everywhere, even if it takes all night. Nobody's getting damn well killed around here."

23

Was Grandpa going to do it? Was he willing to take orders from Flint?

It stayed quiet for a moment, but in the end Grandpa ruffled Kix's hair, pulled on his coat, and called Grandma. She told Grandpa no less than three times to take good care of Kix, and finally Grandpa said, "Of course. And that's why we're going now. Bye."

Moments later, Kix was walking between Grandpa and Flint, who both took exactly the same size steps and were wearing the same kind of boots.

That was a good sign. Why exactly, Kix didn't know. But he breathed in to the bottom of his lungs.

They were going to find Sam.

The lambing shed was one of Sam's favorite spots. That's what Flint said, so they went there to have another look. He swore as he cut open the seal and put the key in the lock.

There was nothing to see there, of course, but Kix still felt very close to Sam because the shed still smelled of the lambs and their hay. He sniffed the way Sam sniffed, his nose in the air.

Flint swore again, and Grandpa said, "Hey. There's a kid here, remember?"

"Sorry," Flint growled. "But I haven't been back in here since it all went to hell."

And when they'd searched the sheep pasture a little later and checked the fields at the other end of the path too, he said, "I guess this means we go into those shitty woods then."

"Hey!" Grandpa said again.

But Flint pulled his cap down further over his head and said, "Yep, into that shitty little forest we go. If he's anywhere, he's in there."

They had to go farther downhill. A ways back behind Flint's house, there was a path past more pine trees with drooping branches, and at the end of that path you went into the forest.

"An hour and a half and you're out the other side," Flint said. "There are slopes and bare patches. Not much of a forest, in other words. But the dog liked it."

He said "the dog." Back when Sam worked on the farm he was named Nanook. Kix didn't think that was a name that suited him, and Flint didn't seem to think so either.

Kix took another deep breath.

"Ready?" Grandpa asked. "It's already late, and it's going to get a lot later. You know that, right?"

Kix nodded.

"There aren't any paths in these woods," Flint said. "We'll take the game trails. The dog would have followed them too. They're like highways — all the wild animals use them. You can tell from the tracks."

Tracks!

They squeezed through a bunch of white pine branches,

and then there they were, standing on a flattened strip that looked just like a path.

It had started snowing again, but there was still no wind, and here in the woods the flakes seemed more like dust.

All that snow lit up the night. The sky was light blue, or maybe light purple. So yes, even if they turned off the flashlights, they would probably still see paw prints. If there were any.

"Won't the tracks fill up with snow?" Kix asked.

Flint grinned. He went down on his knees and gestured for Kix and Grandpa to do the same. "Perfect conditions," he said. "For trackers, at least. The bottom layer of snow is packed hard. It's frozen solid over the last few days. Packed snow is like clay. It captures all the prints, and then it gets hard. Then if you get these loose flakes on top of it, you just do this . . ." He brushed the path with his fingers, sweeping the top layer of snow to one side. "And underneath you've got the tracks. Look. Easy."

"But then we just need to look for Sam's tracks!" Kix said. "And they'll lead us straight to him!"

He looked at Flint. This was the solution — it was easy!

"Yep," Flint said. "If we were trackers. But can you tell the difference between dog tracks and wolf tracks? Or a wolverine's? I can't."

Flint grinned again.

"Grandpa?" Kix asked.

Grandpa shook his head.

For a moment it had seemed simple. A kind of treasure hunt with arrows on the ground. Kix sighed. He asked, "Are there really that many animals here?"

And then Flint did something unexpected. He nodded

at Grandpa, and counted, one, two — and on the count of three they both turned on their flashlights.

"Shh," said Flint. He pointed into the woods, and after a few seconds Kix saw it.

Little lights. All around them. Little green lights. At a distance, true, but not far enough away to be invisible. Flint pointed at his eyes, and Kix understood. All those shining green circles were the eyes of animals.

There were everywhere.

Watching.

Grandpa and Flint turned their flashlights off again.

"Beautiful," Kix whispered.

The animals were keeping a close watch over what these two-legged creatures were doing walking around at night in their domain.

Flint chuckled.

"Sam . . ." Kix whispered. "Maybe they were Sam's eyes too . . ."

But if they were, wouldn't he have come over to them? Because that was how Kix had imagined it: Sam coming up to them with his flag of a tail wagging away, saying hello by groaning for joy.

"No . . ." he whispered to himself. "If Sam saw us now, he'd —"

Halfway through his own sentence he jumped up. "Sam!" he shouted. "Sam! It's me! Here! Sam!"

"Kix," said Grandpa.

But Kix shouted, even louder now, "Sa-am! Sam!"

He stopped yelling and turned his head so that his ears were pointing in the right direction.

No reply. No barking. No whimpering.

Maybe Kix had chased the animals off. Maybe they were just holding their breath. He couldn't hear anything except the quiet falling of snow. And he didn't really hear that either — he just imagined he was hearing it.

Then Grandpa said again, "Kix . . ."

But Flint started walking.

Grandpa waved Kix along. "Follow him. It will all work out."

24

They'd only been in the woods for a couple of minutes when they heard whining.

Flint raised one hand. "Coyotes. But they're a long way off."

They walked on, their boots crunching in the snow. Sometimes one of them sank up to his knees in a hole in the snow and the others had to pull him back out.

"Sam's not scared of coyotes," said Kix.

"Hell no," said Flint.

"No," Kix said, "he watched them until he was sick of it, and then he just barked."

Was Flint laughing? Kix was following a bit behind him, so he couldn't tell for sure.

Kix felt the cold through his mittens, and the tip of his nose was probably already frozen, but he still felt like they were walking around somewhere inside, like they were in an enormous building, a strange building made of trees and frost.

The sounds were soft, and the light seemed to come from left and right and above and below all at once — it was almost cozy.

"Coyotes are a bit like dogs," Grandpa said. "Hyperactive dogs."

"They're nervous wrecks," Flint growled. "But smart. Sometimes when I was out with the dog we'd bump into one that had wandered away from the pack, and then it'd be a stare down. Eyes locked. The two of them. The dog here, and the coyote there."

The dog, thought Kix. Suddenly it sank in: Flint had been together with Sam for ten years. And Kix had only had him for seven months.

"They'd stare at each other," Flint went on, "and they could easily keep it up for a quarter of an hour. You'd see them thinking: *Can I eat him? Can he eat me? Can I use him for something else?* House dogs don't do that, they never think about things. They've turned into lazy creatures, phony animals that wouldn't survive half a day even in a tiny forest like this."

"You're right about that," Grandpa said.

"But not Sam," Kix said. "Sam can survive here."

Flint glanced back at him. He nodded.

And Kix thought: *Seven months. Compared to ten years.* It was a strange thought.

They turned down another path, climbing over fallen trees and every now and then jumping out of the way of packs of snow that came pouring down off the branches.

Kix lost track of the time because Flint was telling more stories about Sam. About the time he spent hours lying next to a sheep that got caught in the undergrowth. And the time a bear had come to the house early one morning and started gnawing on one of Flint's boots, and how Sam had chased him off by barking. And the time he'd come to fetch Flint because one of the horses had slipped and was lying in the mud.

And while Kix was listening to Flint, it seemed like Sam wasn't just nearby in the stories, but in the woods too. As if each step could be the one that brought him into sight: *Hey, Sam, there you are!*

It didn't happen, though. They had been wading through the night for more than an hour, and Kix was starting to get tired, big-yawn tired.

Now and then they stood still. Kix would lean on Grandpa a little, letting the two men discuss which part of the woods they hadn't covered yet. When Grandpa asked, "You alright there, Kix?" Kix made sure to stand up straight again and said, "Yeah, sure, fine."

He kept on calling, "Sam! Sam!" First every twenty steps, then every thirty, and later whenever it seemed right — he'd stopped counting.

Grandpa called out too sometimes, "Sam! Sam!"

And in the end even Flint joined in. Even though he'd never called his dog Sam.

Kix's face got colder and colder, and inside his coat he was getting hotter and hotter. He wanted to go to bed.

Grandpa had already mumbled a couple of times that it was really getting late, but Flint kept on pointing out a new path and a different part of the forest. He said, "We're almost there. We'll find him soon." And Kix repeated it to himself: *We're almost there. We'll find him soon.*

Other thoughts kept on sneaking into his head too.

Because of the stories Flint had told him.

Kix thought they were beautiful, of course he did. He was

90

proud of his dog. But now, deeper into the night, long after the three of them had stopped talking, with them panting from all that stupid plowing through the stupid snow, it was really sinking in that Flint knew a lot more about Sam than Kix did. Sam had lived with Flint a lot longer.

It made Kix feel a bit miserable, Flint's ten years of Sam against his seven months of Sam.

And then Grandpa asked Flint just like that, "Why are you actually doing all this? Why are you helping us?"

At first Flint only blew out a few clouds of steam, but finally he said, "Do you think I haven't missed that dog?"

25

Sam, thought Kix, *why aren't you talking to me?* Surely they'd been down every one of these paths by now?

Flint just kept walking and walking. Grandpa and Kix trudged along behind him, and Grandpa was sure to be feeling just as grouchy as Kix was.

How could Flint have missed Sam? He'd kicked him once, hadn't he, when he was sick in the head? And even if that head of his had gotten better, why were they following Flint so blindly? Wasn't it Kix who had thought that this was where Sam had to be?

Sam, Kix thought, *give me some kind of sign.*

Suddenly Grandpa's phone started ringing. It rang the silence to pieces. It almost hurt your ears.

Grandpa answered it. It was Grandma.

"We're still searching," Grandpa said. "No, not yet . . . Of course I'll look after him . . . As soon as we're done . . . No, not long now."

Not long now. Kix knew that. If they didn't find Sam soon, Grandpa would want to give up. Grandma's voice on the phone already sounded worried and almost angry. It was getting later and later. They weren't trackers, and they'd already searched almost the entire forest.

Sam, thought Kix. *Sam*.

And all at once he had to ask it.

There was no choice. He had to.

Grandpa put his cell phone away, and Kix said, "What if . . . I mean, if he's . . . after all . . . because he was sick . . . and if he's dead . . . where would he . . ."

His sentences were too awful to finish. But Flint understood what he was trying to ask. "Wait a minute," he said.

They stopped. For the first time since they'd come into the woods, Flint pulled off his gloves. He searched his pockets for his cigarettes, tapped one out of the pack, and held it out to Grandpa. Grandpa shook his head. Flint pulled out his lighter and growled when the flame wouldn't start up right away.

Another try, and the glowing red cigarette light was back.

"Okay," said Flint. "Dead. When we've finished searching, we'll have to accept that's a possibility. What old dogs sometimes do is hide. They feel their end coming and crawl off."

He took another puff of his cigarette.

No, no. Kix shook his head hard. No. Sam hadn't crawled off. Sam wasn't planning on dying. But Kix couldn't shut out Flint's words. "Where, then?"

Flint pointed at the trees around them. "Imagine if you had to survive here. At night. Where would you lie down? The snow's not the worst. The worst is the icy wind. So you look for the lowest, deepest spot you can find. I'd say, under a pine. Where the lowest branches form a kind of roof. No snow. No wind. Maybe there's still some moss."

His hand went back up to his mouth for another long drag.

93

Kix looked at Grandpa, and Grandpa nodded. Under the lowest branches of a pine tree.

It made Kix feel sick to his stomach. Maybe they'd walked right past him, Sam dying somewhere under a tree.

Kix was about to throw up. Grandpa noticed and huddled up against him, and Kix felt very small, because if Sam had wanted to hide somewhere, he could be anywhere. Anywhere in this forest. Anywhere in the province. Anywhere in the whole country.

They were here now, but the country was so big you needed a plane to get from one side to the other. And the province was big, and even this forest was pretty big, with lots and lots of trees and lots and lots of spots to die in.

And Kix had thought he was like a little boy in a children's story who could talk to animals. He'd thought he could understand a dog.

Kix took Grandpa's hand. That was something he almost never did. He was too old for it, but now he wanted to feel Grandpa's fingers straight through his mitten, straight through Grandpa's glove.

What were they supposed to do now? Were they going to search the last bit of forest? Would they keep on calling? Or should they start lifting up the lowest branches of the trees until somewhere they found a beautiful, white, dead . . .

Kix was sick, dizzy, everything at once.

And then Grandpa said, "Buddy, if Flint and I thought Sam wasn't with us anymore, do you think we'd be searching like this?"

And Grandpa snapped at Flint, "Did you have to go and say it out loud?"

And Flint threw his cigarette away and said, "He asked, didn't he?"

And Kix heard in his voice that Flint was shocked too
— but just before he was about to finally throw up for real,
Kix heard something. He heard it inside his head, quiet
and weak.

One word. And it was coming from Sam.

Here.

26

"Keep walking," Flint said. "We'll finish searching the woods, then go back to the sheep pasture. If he's dead in a hiding place, then there's no hurry anyway, and in the daylight —"

"He's alive!" Kix shouted.

He was wide awake again. He'd let go of Grandpa's hand. He pulled his cap up a little — he didn't want his ears covered. They had to be free to catch every sound.

"He's alive! I heard him!"

Grandpa wanted to shake his head, Kix saw it, but he didn't give him a chance. "Hurry!" he said, taking a giant step over a pile of snow. For a moment he was about to stumble, but he recovered his footing just in time.

"Kix!" Grandpa called out.

But Kix didn't have a second to lose. "We're close!" he cried, and instead of staying next to Grandpa he was alongside Flint now, then in front of Flint. "Hurry!"

He yelled Sam's name through the freezing night, over and over without stopping. Maybe he was scaring all those animals with their green-dot eyes, but he didn't care.

They stamped through the section of woods Flint said they hadn't covered yet. Kix swiped all the branches he could reach with his arms. It was raining snow. "Sam! Sam! Sam! Sam! Sam!"

And when they'd done the last bit of the woods, they

circled back around to the fields and barns — but they weren't giving up, because Kix heard it again: *Here. I'm here.* Quiet and hidden away in his head.

"Saaaaam!"

They were standing next to the field they'd searched earlier.

Flint said, "I had a snowmobile. That'd come in handy now, but it was sold, of course. We'll have to walk across the field in lines."

"No," said Grandpa. "It's getting too late. We've been everywhere, and we know he's not here. We'll carry on tomorrow, but for now —"

"Grandpa!" Kix cried. "I can really hear him! You don't believe me, but it's true! I can hear him calling me! I know he's here somewhere close by! He says *Here*, and I hear it and . . ."

Kix clenched his fists inside his mittens. They couldn't give up now. Maybe they had to go back into the woods and walk all night if they needed to. Until Kix could hear Sam's voice a little bit louder, a little bit clearer.

Flint stayed silent.

So did Grandpa.

Maybe they were thinking about what Kix had said.

"It's true!" he shouted again. Or rather, he *wanted* to shout it. And Grandpa wanted to say something too, probably something strict, laying down the law — but all of a sudden Flint was acting strange.

He peered into the distance. He frowned. He stepped to one side. He stared past Kix and past Grandpa. He said, "No friggin' way. It can't be . . ." And he started walking.

Kix turned around, and so did Grandpa.

Flint picked up the pace, and Kix shot off after him.

They walked past the field toward Flint's cabin, onto the path through the trees.

Flint was running now, and Kix was racing along behind him. Could he see something there? Was something moving?

Yes — something white, against a stack of wood, and when they got closer Kix's pounding heart leapt straight up into his throat.

Because there, lying on his side, was Sam.

27

Flint got to Sam first, but Kix darted around him. He dropped to his knees, pulled off his mittens, hurled them away, and slid his fingers into Sam's hair.

"Sam, Sam, Sam."

His fairy-tale dog was back, he could hardly believe it, but—"Sam! Sam! Sam!" — he was really here, older than Kix remembered him, thinner, with his coat tangled and dirty, exhausted, unmoving, almost unconscious.

But he was alive.

Kix bent over and pressed his face against Sam's neck. His fingers sought out the places they knew from the days when Sam wanted to be petted for hours on end — *There, Kix, yes, theeeeere* — but now Sam wasn't reacting. Or hardly at all. He did look up through the hair hanging down over his eyes, at an angle, but his eyes weren't sparkling.

"Sam! Sam! Sam!"

Could he see Kix? Could he see Flint and Grandpa, squatting down next to him?

"Incredible," Grandpa said. "Incredible."

"He's alive," Kix said — but Flint suddenly swore.

He stood up and moved around to kneel back down again on the other side of Kix. Next to Sam's head.

He swore again, and Kix's voice broke, "What? What is it?"

Flint didn't answer. Like Kix, he pulled off his gloves, then carefully slid his right hand under Sam's head. He growled, "Light!" at Grandpa, and then Kix saw what Flint had spotted.

There was a needle in Sam's nose.

A sharp, black-pointed needle was sticking out through the top of Sam's muzzle with a thicker, white tube at the bottom. It had forced its way right through Sam's soft nose. And then Kix saw the dried blood around the wound. It was a brown crust, dark brown.

Grandpa was bending over Sam now too. The beam of light moved.

Flint swore for a third time, and Grandpa said, "That's a porcupine quill. Don't touch it. It's got barbs on it. If we mess with it, we'll only make it worse."

Sam had closed his eyes and was lying there quietly panting. A porcupine quill? Had Sam gotten into a fight with a porcupine?

"I could try . . ." Flint said.

"No," said Grandpa. "We'd hurt him. Plus we'd make him panic. I think he's lost some blood, but not too much. By the looks of it, he was lucky."

"I'll get Ormasen to come out," Flint said. "Tomorrow. The vet."

"That'd be best," said Grandpa.

Kix still had his hands buried in Sam's fur. He was confused. Sam wasn't scared of coyotes, and he didn't get into fights with porcupines. Sam knew how to get along with other animals. What had happened? And why was he squatting down next to a motionless Sam in the freezing cold? They should have been jumping around, Sam and him. This wasn't the way to be reunited with the dog you've been missing for weeks.

But Sam had called him. He'd sent a thought out to Kix, and Kix had understood it.

Yes — Kix understood his dog. Otherwise they would never have come here, otherwise they wouldn't be here now. Why wasn't he shouting for joy? Why was Sam being so quiet?

Kix's fingers stopped their petting. "Is he going . . . is he hurt so badly that he . . ."

Grandpa looked startled. He put one arm around Kix and said, "It could be worse, buddy. I don't think he's in that much pain. That quill's been in there a while. Sam's just a bit weak. He's walked for days and days to get here. But he managed it. He's alive, and you found him. And now he needs to drink something."

He said that last bit to Flint, who stood up and grumbled, "And get in out of the cold," and walked over to the cabin.

For a moment Kix sat quietly with Grandpa and his exhausted dog. Kix made sure not to get too close to the wound from the quill. Very carefully, he moved his lips up to his dog's ear and whispered, "Sam! Sam!"

And then he heard a very quiet, *Kix?*

Or maybe not *Kix*, but *Have I made it?*

Kix wasn't sure.

"We'll take care of him," Grandpa said, his comforting arm still wrapped around Kix. "And then we'll call your mom. It's very late, but I think she'll be real glad to hear that Sam's still with us."

Yes. Sam was still with them, and all at once that knowledge flowed down Kix's throat, into his stomach, and through his whole body. It was the opposite of the sick feeling he'd had before. It was a delicious glow that warmed him up from the inside out: Sam was still with them.

28

Flint came outside with a rug. Kix wondered if they were going to leave Sam lying here on the snow, but Grandpa took a corner of the folded rug and carefully slid it under Sam's hind legs. Flint did the same with Sam's front legs.

"Keep him calm, buddy," Grandpa said.

How? Kix thought. *How?* He was still stroking Sam, even though his fingers were now stiff from the cold. And he kept whispering, "Sam, Sam, Sam."

Maybe it helped, because Sam only whined for a moment when Grandpa and Flint lifted him up and laid him on the rug.

"Watch out, kid," Flint told Kix.

Flint and Grandpa then took one end of the rug each, counted to three, and stood up. Sam went up too, into the air on his rug stretcher.

Kix stood up and felt dizzy for a couple of seconds, but Flint and Grandpa were already moving toward the front door. Sam just let it all happen, and that wasn't right either: Sam always decided for himself when and where he was going. And indoors was never where he wanted to be.

"Sam!" Kix said, running after them. Sam turned his head and looked at Kix. Finally! It only lasted a second — after that his eyes closed again — but that was long enough for a message to get through.

It's okay, Sam said.

"Buddy," Grandpa puffed, "the door."

Kix ran past them and opened the front door all the way, kicking a pair of Flint's shoes to one side.

Flint and Grandpa carried Sam in through the hall and into the kitchen, where it was warm.

In the middle of the room, they bent their legs to lower the dog down, and Sam made a soft landing on the floor. Kix was already sitting next to him, hands ready for petting.

29

"Mom!" said Kix.

His fingers were still made of ice, and Grandpa's cell phone felt strange and hard against his cheek.

"Kix!" Mom cried in a faraway voice. "What are you doing there? Your father and I would never have allowed it, but, but . . . you've got Sam!"

After that she started crying.

And then Kix started to cry too, of course.

It felt good to cry for a while, and not childish at all, because it was late at night, and Mom had been wrong about that goodbye song for Sam. He was back, and if that wasn't enough to make you cry, what was?

"I can't believe it," Mom said when she was able to talk again.

"Yes," said Kix.

"It's fantastic," Mom said.

"Yes," said Kix.

"You found him," said Mom, and Kix nodded, because he couldn't just keep saying yes the whole time.

"It really is much too late. Grandpa has to get you to bed right away, but Sam being there, and him still being alive . . ."

She had talked to Grandpa a little bit first and already

knew about the quill in Sam's nose. *It'll be fine*, Grandpa had said, so Kix said that now too, "It will be fine."

And that made Mom start crying again.

Kix passed the phone back to Grandpa. He wanted to be with his dog.

Sam was drinking. Flint had managed that. He'd put some water on a plate so that Sam's nose wouldn't bump against anything, then carefully lifted up Sam's head. Kix had wanted to do it himself, but being able to watch the way a very weak Sam still managed to slurp up some of the water was good too. Slurping was a wonderful sound.

Then Sam slumped back down on the floor, so Kix stroked him some more.

He stroked and stroked and didn't hear what Grandpa said to Mom or what Flint said to Grandpa. He was trying to warm Sam up with his hands, trying to rub him stronger everywhere he could reach, as if he had magic fingers and healing hands.

Suddenly he stood up, walked over to Grandpa, who was still on the phone, felt in the pocket of his coat until he had the car keys, went back outside, opened the rear door of the Chevy, and grabbed his bag. There was something special in it he'd brought from home. He ran back inside, kicked off his boots, and skidded over the wooden floor of Flint's kitchen in his socks until he was back at Sam's blanket. "Look, Sam! Look what I've got."

Kix opened the bag.

Sam didn't look up, but that didn't matter. He'd feel it soon enough, and he'd enjoy it.

"Look, Sam," Kix said again. "Your brush!"

Sam had fallen asleep. Kix had only run the brush over his coat a couple of times. He was trying to be careful, since there were so many tangles.

Flint and Grandpa had tried to get Sam to eat something. At first they'd had a bit of an argument about it.

"Come on," said Grandpa, opening Flint's fridge.

"He's welcome to eat any of it," Flint said, "but I'm telling you, there's no point."

Then it was quiet for a while. Grandpa had whispered something, and Flint had grumbled, and finally they'd gotten out some meat. But Sam was already asleep.

Kix looked at his dog. He was so close. And so real.

I missed you, thought Kix. Those were the kind of words grown-ups used, but he knew it was true. He'd missed him so much.

And I love you, he thought too.

Mom said things like that sometimes, and now Kix was saying them to Sam. Just in his thoughts, true, but that was enough.

Kix's leg started to tingle. He'd been sitting in the same position for a long time.

Flint had stoked up the potbelly stove, so Kix's front was cold and his back was warm. That didn't matter. Nothing besides Sam mattered right now.

Grandpa drank a beer with Flint. Every now and then they checked on Sam and Kix. Sometimes from a distance, sometimes up close. Then they'd lay their hands on Sam's throat and stomach before standing up again.

Time passed, but Kix didn't know how much time. Time didn't count, and neither did words. The things they were saying there at the table were just a jumble to Kix.

That was why he was so shocked when Grandpa suddenly put his hands on Kix's shoulders and whispered, "Buddy, ready to go?"

Go? *Go?*

Kix pretended he hadn't heard. He didn't move.

Grandpa coughed. He knelt down.

Kix could feel Grandpa looking at him.

Kix didn't look back.

"Buddy," Grandpa said again. "Buddy, we're going."

They couldn't. And Kix thought it was so obvious that

they couldn't that he didn't even know if he should shake his head.

"It's late . . ." Grandpa said.

Now Kix shook his head after all.

"Yes, it is," Grandpa said. "We'll come back tomorrow."

Kix still didn't say anything. He just stared straight ahead.

Grandpa stood up. "Kix," he said, louder now, "we're going. Sam is in good hands. And I promised your mother I'd get you to bed."

Kix stood up too.

But he didn't walk to the door. He walked over to the other side of the room.

"Kix . . ." Grandpa said.

Kix had to say something — but he couldn't. How could he leave Sam alone? After all these weeks of searching? After hearing him, understanding him, finding him, and rubbing him warm?

If he left Sam now, it would be like saying, "Bye, Sam, see you again sometime. I'm only a tiny little bit yours. You're only a tiny little bit mine. And who am I leaving you with? Flint. Who's not crazy anymore. So they say. He won't kick you. So they say. He did help search for you, that's true, but he didn't use your name. He called you *The Dog*. And me? Oh, I'm a bit tired. Sorry, Sam, that's much more important."

How could Grandpa think that was even possible?

Kix looked at Sam, and new tears welled up in his eyes.

Then he looked around the room.

Suddenly he knew what to do.

He ran past Grandpa, past Flint.

In the hall he'd seen a little room that he hoped was the bathroom.

Through a door,

through another door,

bang.

Yes, it was the bathroom, and there was a latch. In the rush it slipped out of his fingers a couple of times, but Grandpa and Flint were so surprised that they were still standing in the living room, and he finally got it — he got the door locked in time.

30

Kix pressed his forehead against the bathroom door. Were Flint and Grandpa coming after him?

No, not right now.

Maybe they thought he had to pee. Maybe they thought he wanted to be alone for a moment. To think things through.

Kix looked around. The bathroom wasn't very clean, but it wasn't really dirty either. Some of the tiles were cracked. In the corner next to the toilet, Flint had built a tower of toilet paper rolls.

Kix actually did need to pee.

After flushing, he sat down on the lid of the toilet. Soon Grandpa would come and rattle the door.

What should he say? There was no way he was ever going to leave Sam behind. But it was complicated too. Because what had he thought was going to happen? He hadn't thought anything. Or if he had, he'd thought that he'd find Sam and everything would go back to how it was before. That's what he'd thought. Sam would be back with him and Emilia. With Mom and Dad. With Patriot, Jill, Study, Springer, and Holly. That was how Kix had pictured it all those weeks that Sam was gone. A happy story with a happy ending.

Why wasn't Grandpa coming after him? Was he having another beer?

Kix sighed. It was late, and he was tired, and all at once he felt that.

And would Sam get better? Could Kix be sure that he wouldn't rather have died?

"Kix?"

Suddenly Grandpa was on the other side of the door.

"Are you okay?" Grandpa was asking in his buddy voice.

Kix didn't know what to do. But sitting on the toilet wasn't going to help either. So he straightened his shoulders, flicked up the hook on the door, and stepped out into the hall.

"Grandpa," Kix said. "We can't just leave. I have to stay here with Sam."

Grandpa didn't say a word. He took Kix by the hand, and together they went back into the living room.

"I can't do it." Kix said it again to be sure. "I have to stay with him, and that's what I'm going to do."

Flint was still sitting at the table. He looked at Kix, and at Grandpa, and at their hands.

Kix waited. He'd said enough.

Flint rubbed his cheeks and chin. "Everything okay?" he asked.

"I'm not sure," Grandpa said.

"I'm staying with Sam," Kix said again.

He said it calmly. Because it was something he was completely sure of.

He could still feel Grandpa's hand around his, but if he needed to, he'd lie down on the ground and refuse to move. Then Grandpa and Flint would have to drag him out of the house.

"Kix," Grandpa said, "we heard you. But how can you stay here? Where would you sleep? And if you did . . . I mean . . . If we go home to get some sleep now and drive back first thing in the morning . . . We can make sure we're here before the vet even gets here."

"No," Kix said.

He pulled his hand away and went back to Sam. He bent over his wounded muzzle. The quill looked like it was made of hard plastic, and Sam's nose looked like soft rubber.

Grandpa was just standing there. Maybe he really didn't know what to do next.

But now Flint stood up too.

He walked over to Kix.

I'll run back to the bathroom, thought Kix. *I'll lock myself in again. And I'll grab their car keys, Grandpa's and Flint's. I'll throw them in the toilet and flush them.*

Flint squatted down next to him.

Kix held his breath.

If he touches me, he thought, *I'll give him a karate kick.*

But Flint didn't touch him.

He touched Sam. He laid one hand on Sam's sleeping tummy.

And he said something to Grandpa. He called Grandpa by his first name. Steven. But he was looking at Kix.

Kix looked straight back at him. He wasn't scared.

"Steven," Flint said, "the boy can handle it. He's strong enough. We'll sleep here tonight, close to the dog."

31

Grandpa got the bedroom. He was the oldest, so Flint made him take the bed. "We'll leave the door open," he said. "Then we can listen to your snoring."

"What do you think, Kix?" Grandpa asked.

As far as Kix knew, Grandpa didn't snore, but he was smart enough to realize why they were going to keep the door open. For him. To make sure he was safe.

He nodded.

In the kitchen, Flint put a couple of chairs next to each other. He threw some blankets over them with a pile of sweaters for a pillow.

Kix got real pillows to lie on. Flint put them on the floor next to Sam. Grandpa covered them with a sheet. "Is that okay?" he asked. "Is this what you really want?"

"Yes," said Kix.

Because he was next to Sam, and that was enough.

"Kix?" Grandpa asked again.

"Yes?"

"You do understand, eh? What we're doing here?"

Kix thought that was a strange question. But Grandpa looked really serious.

"Yes," said Kix for the third time. He said it more clearly this time, and in a serious voice.

Grandpa nodded. "Okay, buddy. Call me if you need anything. I'm only ten feet away."

It had all happened pretty fast. Flint and Grandpa had gone out into the hall together and had an argument. Kix had heard them at it. But it hadn't taken long. When they came back into the kitchen, Grandpa shrugged and shook his head. But after that he'd still called Grandma once more, and Mom too. They had a whole lot of questions, and Grandpa had a whole lot of answers. They were angry at him — of course they were — but in the end Grandpa said, "My battery's almost dead. I promise, I'm right here with him. I'll keep an eye on it all. I'll call back in the morning."

Kix hadn't brushed his teeth. He didn't have any pajamas to wear, so he just kept on his T-shirt, sweater, pants, and socks. But he was with Sam.

Grandpa rubbed Kix's cheeks with his hands, which felt hard and soft at the same time, and then Kix lay down, yawned, and said, "Grandpa, look at Sam."

Sam's breathing was calm and quiet. As if he knew that everything was going to be fine, that he was safe now that Kix was sleeping next to him.

Then Grandpa lay down on the creaky bed, and Flint turned off the lights.

As soon as Kix's head touched the pillow, his eyes fell shut.

But his ears were still open.

His ears heard Grandpa turning over in bed. They heard the wind that had picked up outside. They heard the kitchen faucet dripping. Sometimes, briefly, and then not for a long while.

Coughing too. That was Flint. Caused by smoking, of course.

The sounds kept Kix's thoughts awake. And there were smells too. The smell of Flint's floor boards. The blankets he'd been given that smelled like someone had put them away at the bottom of a dresser a long time ago. And Sam. That was a wet smell, but also an old smell.

How could Kix be so sleepy, yet not asleep?

It was strange to be lying on the floor. But it was a nice kind of strange. *Now,* Kix thought, *I'm closer to my dog than ever before.* And that made him smile. He felt the corners of his mouth sliding up, and that was the last thing he remembered, because after that he didn't smell or hear or think anything for quite a while.

Quite a while.

Later — how much later? — there was movement next to him. Sam's leg lashed out. His nails clicked on the floor. A dream. A dog dream.

Kix surfaced briefly from his sleep too, but as soon as Sam went quiet again, dozing on, breathing calmly, Kix too sank back onto his pillows.

Sometime in those hours, Kix dreamed about something that had really happened a few months earlier.

It had been late at night, and Kix had heard his father come home. Suddenly there was a racket, an unfamiliar racket — and laughter. Dad's. Then he called out to Mom, "Sarah! Sarah! Quick, come here!"

He heard the laundry room door bang, and then Mom started laughing too, "Springer!" she cried. "Oh, no!"

Kix rushed to get his slippers on and ran to the garage, where he saw Springer trembling in a corner and smelled a nasty, pungent smell, a smell that forced its way right up his nose.

"Kix," Mom said, "keep that door shut. Springer just met a skunk."

A skunk had come to the farm — that happened ev-ery now and then. When Dad came home, Springer had escaped from the garage, seen the skunk, and thought, *Hey, someone to play with!* Because that was what Springer always thought about everyone. She'd bounded over to the skunk, which turned around and *psssshhhhhttt!*

They spent the rest of the night washing Springer. They had to do it right away, four times in a row with special shampoo, in order to get rid of that horrible stench.

But the funniest thing was Sam sitting by the open garage door. He was chuckling. Sam sat there the whole time with a friendly look on his face, quietly laughing at Springer.

And it was as if Sam was trying to say, *I warned her, Kix. But you and I don't mind, do we? We're not going to get upset about a bit of stink. Not on our Springer.*

It was a nice memory, and a nice dream. From the days when there was nothing wrong with Sam. But then Kix woke with a start.

It was still the middle of the night, and he stared straight ahead with his eyes open wide.

He'd heard a new sound.

A frightened sound.

32

It wasn't something Grandpa or Flint had heard. They might not have been snoring, but they *were* asleep, because their breathing was heavy and drawn out.

Kix raised himself up on his elbows. Yes, he had heard something, but it was a sound that almost didn't exist.

Sam was squeaking under his breath. Very quietly.

It was hard to see Sam's eyes in the dark, but Kix knew what they looked like. Like he was surprised. Confused. Nervous.

"Sam," Kix whispered, "I'm here, it's okay."

But he got up and moved closer, because Sam was about to start howling.

The kind of howling that started with quiet squeaking. And soon it would be yowl-howling like that time at home when they'd built a little palace in the garage for Sam, and he hadn't wanted to be king.

Kix was sure of it. And he wanted to prevent it, he wanted Sam to understand that he understood him, so he rubbed Sam's back and said, "Come with me."

Sam stood up.

He didn't do it easily. His legs were still worn out from his long journey.

Kix whispered, "Come on, boy. Here."

Very quietly, he opened the door to the hall. Sam wobbled through.

Kix closed the door again. Sam's hair brushed against the wall.

Quickly and quietly, Kix pulled on his coat. And his boots. "Come on, Sam."

He opened the front door.

Of course Sam wanted to howl. He'd woken up and seen where he was — inside a house — and that was somewhere he didn't want to be.

Now he was standing on the small porch.

He sniffed the air. The moon was still reflecting white light over the countryside. Although it wasn't snowing anymore, it felt really icy in the wind. But Kix wasn't worried about that now. He was watching Sam, who was going down the steps slowly and carefully, still weak. And when Sam put his paws on the snow, Kix caught something again. One short sentence. It woke him up even more and brought a big grin to his face.

This is good, Sam said.

Kix knew that Sam wouldn't run away.

Sam took a few steps to the left and lay down between the steps and Flint's woodpile. It was sheltered there, and yet as close to Kix as possible.

Sam said, *Here. I'm here.*

At least that was what Kix understood. The words were hidden in a contented howling noise.

"Wait a sec," Kix said, "I'll be right back."

He crept back inside, grabbed his pillow and blanket, and curled up on the narrow porch, just above Sam and, like him, out of the wind. Kix pulled on his mittens, took his cap out of his coat pocket, and wrapped the blanket around his shoulders.

33

Cold air feels good in your nose.

Kix thought it was strange he hadn't thought of that earlier that night.

"Sam," he said quietly to make sure he didn't wake them up inside, "how's the quill?"

No answer.

"The vet's coming tomorrow."

Sam grunted.

"We went to see Choca. You'd been there too."

Sam didn't say anything, but he was listening. Kix was sure of it.

"When you weren't at Choca's and we couldn't find you, everybody thought we'd never see you again. But not me. And then Grandpa said that you were like a puppy again. And suddenly I figured it out. You wanted to go back to the old days. Because that's what puppyish dogs do, and so do puppyish people. They don't remember anything about now, but they still know everything about when they were little. And that's how I found you. And then you called me too, and Flint helped, and . . ."

Just then something terrible happened.

Not to Sam — he'd gone back to sleep, quietly, in his beautiful spot without a stove and without any walls — but to Kix.

Suddenly he wasn't wearing his coat anymore, and he didn't have the blanket wrapped around him. His heart and stomach, his throat and veins all filled with cold, because suddenly he realized how stupid he'd been. He'd made a big mistake, a mistake he only now saw: *if Sam wanted to go back to the old days, he didn't want to come back to now.*

That was what it came down to.

Sam wanted to be here.

He had said so himself. *I'm here. It's good.*

Sam had walked here. Through the snow, through the cold. He had walked all that way, wearing out his knees and freezing his paws. He'd done it because he wanted to be in the place he could picture most clearly now that he'd started getting puppyish.

This place.

Not to die. No — to live again in the past.

And now the freezing nighttime wind was blowing on Kix's ears, and that was because he'd suddenly thought of something else: Sam couldn't go back to Kix's house no matter what. Sam couldn't go in a car!

"Sam can't go in a car!"

Maybe Kix said it out loud. Maybe he was crying too. He was shivering a bit anyway, and then he was startled.

Because something was tossed on top of him, and wrapped around him.

Another blanket.

Kix looked over his shoulder nervously.

It was Flint. The man he was going to lose his dog to.

34

Flint had woken up and come outside, and Kix hadn't heard him at all. But Flint didn't say anything. He looked at Kix and then over the edge of the porch at Sam.

Kix was staring numbly into space.

He heard Flint go back into the house and come back out again. With a coat. With a cap. With a scarf.

He sat down next to Kix and started talking.

He said, "Can too."

Kix didn't understand what Flint was talking about.

"He can too," said Flint. "He can go in a car. If you like I'll take him straight back to that house of yours. With the horses."

Kix swallowed. He really didn't understand what Flint was talking about. "Horses?"

"Yeah," Flint said. "At your place. Horses."

What was Flint talking about? Taking him back?

"I don't get it," whispered Kix.

"Okay," said Flint.

And after that he said, "I don't have any tea."

And then he was silent again.

"Otherwise I'd have made some."

Kix thought, *Tea?*

"It's almost four in the morning," said Flint. "But we'll

be here for a while. That's why tea would be good. But I haven't got any."

Kix finally got his voice back. "In a car?" he asked.

It sounded a bit feeble, even to Kix.

"Oh, hell yeah," said Flint, who lit a cigarette. "That dog's just crazy about going for rides. You must have noticed that."

"What?" said Kix. "No."

Flint broke out in a coughing laugh. "That old man of yours must drive the wrong kind of car."

"Sam doesn't like cars."

"Sure he does."

"No."

"Course he does. He always lies down in front of 'em, doesn't he? You're not telling me he's stopped doing that."

"In front of the car? Yeah, but that means —"

"That he wants to get in. His own way too, of course! I always had to open the back door and politely ask him if he would please get into the vehicle. Window open and nose in the breeze. Oh, yeah. He loved it."

Kix frowned.

Had they misunderstood him the whole time? Sam didn't lie down in front of cars because he wanted to stop them from leaving. Or because his brain was getting fuzzy. He wanted to go for a ride! And they'd never figured it out. Not even Kix.

Kix stretched a little and looked down at the dog he might not have understood after all.

Sam was still asleep. His stomach was moving up and down with each breath. The quill through his nose was moving slightly to the same rhythm. Kix sank back on his pillow. The second blanket had slid down. Flint clamped the cigarette between his lips, bent over Kix, and pulled the blanket back up.

Kix didn't want Flint near him, so he slid over a little. He pulled his cap down further over his forehead and sank as low as he could into his collar until only his nose was sticking out into the cold. That was better.

This was where he wanted to be. With Sam. If he wanted to, he could go inside to Grandpa. He could even curl up next to him in the warm bed. He could ask him to drive away from here. If Sam really loved cars that much, Kix could open the back door of the Chevy. He could invite Sam to get in — "White wonder-dog Sam, would you like to go for a ride? We've got a vet, too. You know her."

He could do that.

Flint wouldn't stop him.

Maybe Kix hadn't always understood his dog that well. But he understood Flint. Pretty much. Flint was sitting here now. More or less keeping watch. Over him. And over Sam. He'd brought out an extra blanket, and he'd made sure that Kix could stay here tonight to sleep next to Sam. No, Flint wouldn't stop him. But his head still felt so heavy.

So Kix stayed sitting there a little longer.

The wind had died down and all three of them were still. Kix and Flint and Sam.

Kix sat brooding in his coat. His stomach had started aching, and it wasn't because of the cold.

Suddenly the question was there.

Kix turned to look at Flint. The material of his coat rustled, and he heard himself say, "Why did you do it?"

Flint knew right away what Kix meant. He'd probably been expecting the question for a while.

It was something Kix had never understood. If Flint had really loved Sam, why had he kicked him?

Flint took three drags off the butt of his cigarette, flicked it away past the other side of the porch, and said, "You're asking how I could get it into my filthy head to threaten my own dog?"

"Sam," said Kix.

"Yeah," said Flint. "Sam. How's he doing down there anyway?"

He gestured with his chin at the spot where Sam was lying.

"Good," said Kix.

"Breathing calmly?"

"Yes," said Kix. "Why'd you do it?"

35

Flint sniffed. Every noise sounded louder tonight, but when he finally started talking, his voice was soft. Kix had to hold his breath and turn his head so he didn't miss anything.

"I spent more than fifteen years working on a ranch. Horses, cattle. Bouncing over the fields in a jeep, herding the cattle, rounding them up, branding them, working hard. I lived there, too, and I was surrounded by animals, so you could say, what'd I have to gripe about? The boss was a stingy bastard, but I was sixteen when I started, and I stuck it out. And then one of my grandfathers died. Suddenly I inherited some money. When I heard about it, I was at a livestock market, and I'd just seen a couple of Scottish Blackfaces — they're sheep. I saw them and I thought, I'll make some inquiries. The dealer sang their praises, said they'd never ever get sick. And they can graze rough country, and you sell the wool, of course, but the horns too, because they use 'em to make walking sticks. That's what that guy said. Man, he was smooth. Is this too much detail, kid?"

"No," said Kix. "Scottish Blackfaces."

"Exactly," said Flint. "To cut a long story short, six months later I left the ranch. I bought this place here. The house was a dump, but I fixed it up and built the sheds and this cabin too, for visitors. I thought, then I can rent it out to city folk. I got my first sheep from that guy from the market, and then I was a farmer. My parents stabled a few horses here. And I muddled along for a while, and after a year or two I had myself a proper little farm."

"And Sam?" said Kix.

"Sam . . ." said Flint. "He chose me."

Flint stopped telling his story for a moment and patted his coat pocket. Maybe he was already looking for another cigarette.

Kix had heard him right: Sam chose Flint. So it had been like that with him too. Sam had done the choosing then as well. Sam decided for himself where he wanted to live. Kix felt another twinge of pain in his stomach and looked down from the porch. At Sam. Still fine.

"How?" he asked.

Flint didn't stick another cigarette in his mouth after all. He continued his story. "There were four of them. White puppies. Five or six weeks, no older. I'd driven a long way for them, 'cause I had my heart set on a Pyrenees. They're hard workers, and they have a mind of their own. They're independent.

"So I'm checking out the litter. Three of them are squirming around, and one of them is sitting up straight, like the king of the damn castle, and looking at me. And I don't want you to laugh, kid, but I swear: he talks to me. Not really talking. Not out loud. But still. I look him in the eyes, and I can understand him. He says, *Here I am. I'm here.*"

Kix froze. So Sam had spoken to Flint too!
Here I am, he'd said. *Here I am.*
And Flint had understood.
"It used to happen to me a lot too," Flint went on. "I understood him. I don't have to tell you what those eyes do to you. He's got a whole world inside of those eyes. They know a lot more than you and I can see.
"You said earlier tonight that you'd heard him calling. Sam, I mean. And then I thought, this kid gets it. I felt that last summer too, on that rotten night, remember? But now, tonight, I realized that I'd met the first person who wouldn't send me back to the loony bin when I say that my dog talked to me."

Kix knew he had to say something. But he couldn't manage it.
He nodded slightly, and he felt a fever building up inside his head.
Flint understood Sam too.
Flint was just like him.
"Anyway," Flint said, "I loved my farm. It was tough, but I slogged away at it. I would have been happy to get up in the middle of the night every night to help birth a lamb. I could have spent the whole year wandering the hills with

my flock. I had even less time to myself than I did on the ranch, but they were the best years of my life. And that dog was always with me. He always showed me the way. That dog gave me advice — it was as simple as that. It's a foolish thing to say, but I'm a fool. I never called him by his name because he was everything to me. He was The Dog, with a capital T and a capital D, get it? I don't need to explain it to you. You understand. Otherwise you'd be at home asleep, dreaming about your Power Rangers, or whatever it is kids play with these days."

Something glowed in Kix's head, but it wasn't a fever. It glowed and hurt. Kix picked up his pillow and went down the steps with the blankets around his shoulders. He walked over to Sam and laid the pillow down as close to him as he could. Then he sat down on it with his back against the porch. He pulled the blankets tight around him until it was like he was inside a tent.

Flint? He could do whatever he liked. Kix stared at Sam, and kept staring at Sam.

From the corner of his eye he could see that Flint wasn't getting up to come and sit next to him. But he did slide over on the steps. He was a bit closer now.

The glow inside of Kix glowed brighter, and he knew that there was more to come. Did he want to hear it? He didn't know. Yes. No.

"Kix," Flint said, and that was the first time he'd said "Kix" and not "kid" or "toddler." "Kix," he said, "I'm asking a lot of you. But you'll understand, I'm sure of it. This is a night that's not like any other, and if it gets to be too much for you, you let me know. But I want to tell you, because soon it'll be light and then . . ."

He hesitated for a moment. "Well, then this night will be over."

Flint was wrong. Kix didn't understand him at all. Except that bit about the night not being like any other. He understood that.

"Go on," he said quietly. Hoarsely. Across Sam's back, in Flint's direction.

36

"Things started going wrong with the farm. Money problems. New regulations. And the herd got a disease after all — boils. I got that under control pretty fast, but the sales of the yearlings were down — the new lambs, I mean. I made mistakes too. I had a kind of girlfriend then, but she left me. Everything went wrong. I lost it all.

"They came with cattle trucks. Bucks gone, ewes gone, lambs gone. They took my horses away too. I sat here and watched it happen. The dog tried to chase those guys off, barking at them, but he was way out of his depth. I remember trying to call him over to me because I thought they might hurt him. I was so mixed up . . .

"My mother was inside packing up my stuff. I swore and ran around the place, but they were already driving off. The barn was sealed shut. But the worst thing was that the dog was going crazy from his own barking and whining, and I couldn't understand him. I hadn't for a while. Nothing was getting through to me, you know what I mean? Not a single sentence, no feelings. The line was dead, and looking back it had been like that for at least half a year. I'd lost my dog too, in other words. That's what I thought.

"Anyway — I lost it. He was going nuts, and I couldn't stand it anymore. I screamed at him, but he didn't even notice me. And then I leapt at him because I just wanted him to be quiet. I wanted him to give me a sign that it was okay. That we'd carry on together. But no sign came. He was desperate, and I was desperate. In the end it was my mother who found me there. I . . ."

It was as if the nasty Flint was back again. The Flint that Kix was scared of. Not because he was doing scary things, but because Kix could picture him lashing out at Sam. Kicking him. This Sam, right next to him. How could he — how *could* he have done that?

Just the thought of it made Kix groan. "But how could you . . ." he whispered, and his voice broke. "How could you kick . . ."

"I know," said Flint quietly, very quietly. "I was crazy. I'm not justifying it, because . . . wait, did you say 'kick'?"

"Yes."

"No!" Flint said. "I didn't kick him. Did you really think I kicked him? I threatened him and I yelled at him, that's bad enough. But I never laid a finger on him, and I definitely didn't kick him! Do you actually think I'd hurt my dog? No! No! Ask my mother, I never . . ."

Kix almost felt crazy now too. It was as if someone was shaking his glowing head. So Flint hadn't kicked Sam? Really?

"I scared him!" Flint was talking louder and louder. "The dog didn't recognize me anymore, and he cowered away. I can't get that picture out of my head. But I never laid a finger on him, of course not!"

All at once Flint turned his head away. To the side of the house where there was only night.

So he hadn't kicked him.

Flint turned back again. He looked at Sam. And then at Kix.

"But it doesn't matter," he said softly. "I betrayed his trust in me. I saw it in his eyes. He didn't know who I was anymore, and it drained the life out of him. It went out like a candle. I saw it happen."

Kix wanted to get away.

He wanted to fall asleep and dream his way back in time. Mr. Jones from across the road had told Dad that Flint had gone crazy. And then Grandpa had heard from someone else that Flint had kicked his dog. But that hadn't been true. He'd never kicked him.

Now Kix had to touch Sam. He started petting him. With his mittens still on. Through his mittens.

A shiver went through Sam's body, but he didn't wake up.

And then Kix was suddenly able to talk again.

"Sam's old," he said. "His brain is starting to wear out."

"Your grandfather told me," said Flint. "He said it's been getting worse and worse too. Maybe it's been happening a while, eh? Maybe that's why he stopped talking to me. What do you think? When I was in the hospital I thought about him all the time. I thought that I'd made him go silent in his head. Feeling guilty, kid, that's the worst. I did it all wrong. Even if it was just old age, his old-dog-old-age . . ."

Flint stopped talking for a moment.

Kix sat there and waited . . . and waited.

Flint coughed and said, "I'm getting a second chance here. The bank's thinking about letting me buy a few new sheep. I've been doing some jobs in the area, and I seem to be getting it back together. But . . ."

Suddenly there was a low voice. A stern voice.

Grandpa was standing in the doorway.

"Flint!" he roared. "It's the middle of the night, dammit! What do you think you're doing, you numbskull? What's gotten into you?"

And then to Kix, "You're going to get your butt back into bed right away!"

Grandpa was mad at Flint, and Flint shrank a little.

But Kix stood up. And speaking to the night sky over the farm, he said, "Sam came here! By himself! Back to Flint!"

Kix pulled up his blankets, which had slipped down to his feet, turned around to Flint, and shouted, "Back to you! He came back to you!"

Then he threw the blankets to Flint, at Flint, and ran past him up the steps, past Grandpa too. He shoved the door open, stormed into the house, raced to the bedroom, and dove into the bed. He buried himself under the blankets with his boots on, his coat on, his cap, his scarf, his clothes on. He hid himself as far down as possible, in the hollow that had to be there somewhere, deep in the bed, a dark place to get away, escaping from all the things that had glowed together in his head to make something he was sure of.

And now a flood of tears came pouring out of his eyes. He cried softly, but nobody heard it because he was gone, tired, empty — he'd disappeared.

He was running away from something that couldn't be any other way. From something that Flint's story had made perfectly clear.

Flint had never kicked his dog.

Flint had given his dog to him, to Kix.

Because in the summer Flint had realized that Sam had chosen Kix.

But now it was the other way around.

Now Sam had chosen Flint.

So Flint could start over again.

And that was why.
That was why Kix had to give Sam back again.
Now.
In winter.
To Flint.

37

When Kix woke up the next morning, he wasn't lying in a dark hole anymore. The first thing he felt was the sun on his cheek. The second was the pillow under his ear.

Grandpa! He'd slept right next to him, hadn't he?

It smelled strange here. Everything was strange here. He got out of bed and couldn't see anyone. It must have already been late because the light coming in through the windows was clear, bright sunlight.

Sam! Sam!

The moment Kix thought of his dog a bolt of pain shot through him.

He remembered now. Yesterday evening. Last night. He had to give Sam back.

Kix picked his way through the hall. That's where his boots and coat were. Grandpa must have taken them off last night. He put them on, even though he wasn't sure he wanted to go outside. He didn't even know if he wanted to see Sam.

Just thinking about his dog hurt. His dog's name hurt — no, no, no. Not *his* dog anymore.

He opened the front door anyway. He couldn't just stay inside.

Dazzling sparkles reflected off the snow, and Kix squeezed his eyes shut. Slowly they adjusted to the open space, outside on Flint's farm.

It looked different in the daylight. Bigger. More real.

"Kix! Buddy!"

Grandpa appeared from behind a row of trees. Flint was walking along beside him. Apparently they'd made up again after Grandpa's angry words last night. Kix watched as they came toward him, both smiling.

Walking between them was Sam.

His tail was wagging low to the ground.

But it was wagging.

It was wagging!

"You missed the vet," Grandpa said. "He was a real pro. He had the quill out before we knew it. With just a light anesthetic. Sam didn't even bark. He lay still for a while afterwards, but look at him now. It looks like he's planning to have a good day today!"

Kix looked at Sam's nose. It was hardly even swollen.

But Kix's pain hadn't disappeared. There were about a hundred quills in his chest.

Grandpa came over next to him. He wrapped his big arm around Kix's shoulders — and Kix started to cry.

He cried like a little kid. Like he was two or three. Like a toddler.

Grandpa was shocked, and couldn't do anything except take Kix inside, sit down at the table, and pull him up onto his lap. Kix hadn't been able to keep himself from crying, and now he couldn't stop crying either.

Sam had stayed outside. Still wagging his tail, maybe.

Kix couldn't even talk.

Flint, who'd followed them in, put a glass of water on the table in front of him. After quite a few minutes and quite a few gulps of water, Kix was able to get his breathing back under control.

The two men looked at him quizzically.

They didn't understand him, so he explained it to them as best he could. About the decision. And the truth.

That Sam was a dog who decided for himself where to live. And now he wanted to be with Flint. On his old farm. Because Flint could talk to him too. And Sam talked back. And Sam had forgotten all about that almost-kick a long time ago, because why else would an old dog walk all those miles to get here? And maybe he was forgetful, and maybe he didn't know how to get along with porcupines or skunks anymore, and maybe . . .

Kix didn't know what to say next and started crying again. "Maybe we can come to visit," he said in a thin, shaky voice, "when I'm staying at Grandma and Grandpa's anyway . . ."

At that Grandpa banged his fist on the table.

Hard.

The glass fell over. The bit of water Kix hadn't drunk yet spilled, leaving a dark patch on the wood.

Grandpa's voice wasn't nearly as deep as usual when he hit the table again and shouted, "What? HAVE YOU GONE COMPLETELY NUTS? Yes — the dog walked here. And yes — maybe the dog wanted to go back to the old days. But they're gone! Do you see any sheep here? You see any horses? Flint's going to try to build his farm back up again, okay, and if I know this stubborn old cowboy, he'll do it too, but it will be different. What's gone is gone. The old days never come back. Sam is too old to be young again. Even if he wants to chase after wolves, he can't. What Sam needs is two kids, two grown-ups, two other dogs, and a bunch of horses. But especially those two kids. You'll pet him and pet him and pet him again and brush him and comb him and put braids in his hair if you want to, whatever you like. You know what the vet said? Just here, just now? 'This is a tough old dog. And with love and attention, he can last a good while yet.' Love and attention, you hear me?"

Grandpa had started talking a bit quieter, but now he yelled: "AND WHO'S GOING TO GIVE HIM LOVE AND ATTENTION BETTER THAN THE BOY WHO'S SAVED HIS DARN LIFE, NOT ONCE BUT TWICE?"

Kix gasped. His heart pounded hard inside his chest.

Grandpa shouted as if he was about to box Kix's ears. But he didn't do that, of course. He never did anything like that. But Kix still felt suddenly as if it had happened, as if Grandpa had boxed his ears.

"What?" he whispered. "What?"

"That's right!" Grandpa said. "Saved his life twice. Once on that stupid night with those stupid guns. Flint told me all about it just this morning when I apologized to him for thinking he'd kicked Sam. And the second time you saved his life was last night, of course."

"What?"

"Don't you understand?" Grandpa growled, softly now, "If you hadn't found him, and if you hadn't watched over him afterward, he would have . . . Flint and I, we both thought his last hours had come. That he wouldn't live through the night. But you pulled him through. That dog kept fighting because you were there next to him. Because he wanted to stay with you.

"That's right — don't look so surprised. Didn't you get it? I didn't want you to see your dog die. That's why I thought we should go home. But Flint here said you could take it. He apparently understands nine-year-old dog-boys. Probably because you're just as stubborn as he is."

Kix stared at the water stain on the table. His cheeks were burning.

Sam's last hours? Why hadn't he figured out what Grandpa and Flint were thinking?

All these thoughts were making his head spin. Had Sam really almost died? But he wasn't dead! He was walking around outside wagging his tail! Was that because of him? Could Sam go home with him after all? Was that the best thing to do? Had Sam decided to walk here when he was all fuzzy and forgetful inside his head? Was he too old now to decide for himself where to live? Did the people who were able to protect him have to do that for him — just like with old people whose heads were full of riddles?

And was he, Kix, the person who was best able to protect him?

Kix looked up cautiously.

At Flint.

At the man with the sad eyes, who was going to lose his dog now for the second time.

But Flint's eyes weren't sad.

They were gleaming.

"Listen, kid," he whispered in his creaky voice, "after Ormasen pulled that quill out this morning, it was like a miracle how fast your dog started to recover. And it *was* a miracle, because you know what happened? He talked to me. I could understand him again. For the first time since I don't know when, for the first time in ages. And he only said one word. Ten times in a row. No, not a word, a name. *Kix*. That was it. *Kix. Kix. Kix.*"

Kix's legs banged against the tabletop. He jumped off Grandpa's lap, ran over to the living room door, threw it open, ran through the front door, and leapt off the porch. Without checking to see if Grandpa or Flint were following him, he swung his head left and right. Where was Sam?

Where was his dog?

He ran past the row of trees on the side of the yard, looking for the path through the pines, and then he found it. Where was Sam? Was he at the farmhouse? Near the sheds? In the sheep pasture?

Kix flew over the snow until he found him and there, around the side of the big house, he dropped down next to him. On his knees.

Sam was lying comfortably in the cold sun. Kix sighed, "Sam!" He ran his fingers through that long, damp, white wonder hair. He pressed his nose against Sam's neck and

wanted to say all kinds of things. About mysteries, about staying alive, about going home, about playing at the campground, about the dogs and the horses, but he didn't say any of it, because Sam was already saying something.

Sam said what Flint had said Sam had said.

Kix. Kix. Kixkixkix.

And only then did Kix notice where Sam was lying.

In front of the car.

Grandpa's car.

Kix helped Flint straighten up the bedding. He asked, "Are you going to get a new dog? You'll need one, won't you, if you're going to have sheep again?"

"I suppose," Flint said. "Will you come and help me pick one out?"

"Sure," said Kix. "I'd like to."

Grandpa called Grandma. "We're on our way," Kix heard him say.

But after stopping to see Grandma, they were going to keep going. Home. With hot chocolate on the way and, *and* . . . Sam sniffing in the back of the Chevy!

Kix wanted to run around and knock all of the snow off the pine branches. Only now could he really believe it. Now that they were almost in the car.

Almost.

It was going to be difficult. From now on Kix would have to look after Sam twice as well to make sure he didn't wander off again. He wasn't sure yet how he was going to do that. No, it wouldn't be easy. Grandpa had told him so, and Flint had said the same. The riddles in Sam's head would only get bigger, not smaller. And they didn't know how much longer Sam would live, either. "But," they said, "if anyone can look after him, it's you."

What's more, Flint was going to be visiting his parents more often, their neighbors across the road, Mr. and Mrs. Jones. And when he was there, he could easily drop in, couldn't he? Then Sam would see his old master again, and that would be sure to help. Wouldn't it?

Kix couldn't think straight right now. He just wanted to yell and jump around.

He didn't though. He stayed where he was, next to Grandpa. Because Grandpa was dialing Mom's number. He handed the phone to Kix. "Watch out," he said, "your mom's bound to still be angry."

But it wasn't Mom who answered the phone. It was Emilia.

She immediately started to chatter away about her cousins. About making necklaces and puppet shows and all the things they'd done yesterday.

Kix didn't have any patience for it.

"Emilia!" he shouted in the middle of one of her sentences. "Shut up for a second! We've got a lot of brushing to do. Tomorrow. You and me. Sam can't decide where he belongs, and that's why we've decided for him. Emilia, do you hear what I'm saying? It's really true, so you have to go and tell everyone! Sam's back, and I'm bringing him home!"

A Note from the Author

Sam's story began in the summer, when he decided that he wanted to live with my brother's family. Their house is in Canada, and at the time I happened to be visiting. The story was so special that I just had to write a book about it. That book became *A Dog Like Sam*.

But after I'd returned home to Holland, the story continued. All through fall and winter, my brother René, his wife Karen, and their children kept sending me updates. And again, so much happened with Sam, and they were such special things that I had to write a book about it. A second book.

That's the book you've just read.

Sam really does exist — there's a photo of me with him on the next page.

While writing this book, I had a lot of help from Karen Christie and René van de Vendel, and I've dedicated this book to them and to their children: Nicolette, Anthony, Matthew, and Anna. I also want to thank Karen's parents, Jaimie and Marilynn Christie.

Special thanks to Beorn Nijenhuis, who told me about things like the way coyotes act when they encounter something unfamiliar.

Lastly: the song that Kix's mother listens to is "So Long, Old Friend" from the TV film *Here Comes Garfield*. You can find it on YouTube.

And the Bunnicula book Kix and his mom are reading is called *Bunnicula: A Rabbit-Tale of Mystery* by Deborah and James Howe.

Edward